A Dream to Build a Kiss On

By
Narrelle M Harris

Illustrations By
Caroline Jennings

Paperback ISBN 978-0-9935136-8-8
ePub ISBN 978-0-9935136-9-5

Published in the UK by Improbable Press Limited
71-75 Shelton Street, Covent Garden, London, WC2H 9JQ

To the Pixies, with love.

-- Narrelle M Harris

To my family.

~ Caroline Jennings

1. The End, or the Beginning

The army base is in a plateau. Arid, sandy. Green along the rivers, beige everywhere else. It has uncanny beauty, punctuated by sudden violence.

Captain John Watson's Afghanistan is more than sand and bombs. He fills his sketchbook with wide blue skies hung on rocky peaks; sunsets kissing the horizon; kestrels on the wing; red foxes; white goats; a porcupine; children playing with rag balls and kites.

At Nad Ali patrol base, John's Afghanistan is service. It's finally feeling he *belongs*.

But today. Oh, *today*.

Doctors once died in war here, with their comrades, 140 years ago: at the battles of Ali Masjid, Sherpur, Maiwand. In today's Afghanistan, a doctor shouldn't be crouched in the dirt over a wounded driver while bullets spit around them.

Doctor Watson went with his evac team to meet the medical convoy. The terrain should've been secure. Now he's trying to save a life; trying not to die, while some lone bastard chooses *one more battle*.

John tries to drag his patient to safety.

A bullet breaks his shoulder open.

He spins.

Blood sprays.

He

falls.

"Trixie's down!" Blue shouts.

Pain.

Pain.

Pain.

John gasps in the dirt. So alone, far from home.

He thinks of Hugh. Is sorry/not sorry.
He thinks of Alice. Weeps.
So alone.
His life seeps away in an ebbtide of blood.

2. The Musgrave Ritual

Sherlock Holmes is a man of reason, but like anyone, he has rituals.

After a case, he writes its clinical autopsy; a work of pure logic. Next, his personal journal: his fears and satisfactions. How he failed. How to improve. Rituals complete, Sherlock seeks new challenges.

When they're too long coming, he has another ritual.

From a box in his desk, he takes his syringe and fresh needle. Places them on the table with the last dose of cocaine.

He hasn't needed them for four years, 87 days.

He asks six questions.

Did I do enough? Did I help someone? Hurt anyone?

Did I let their opinion of me matter?

Does it prove Reggie right if I did?

Do I care if it does?

Sherlock told his brother that the cocaine was about boredom. A half truth.

Does Mycroft know what Musgrave did? Said?

In the early days of this ritual, Sherlock would remember kissing Reggie. Being kissed. No more.

Love is useless. Deceptive. Damaging.

Today, caseless, he lays out the solution to his old problem. He asks and answers, according to the ritual. The last answer is always the same.

Obviously, since here I am.

Choose.

Syringe, cocaine, questions, go back in the drawer.

Four years, 88 days.

He hopes there's a case tomorrow.

Sherlock can't bear to be banal.

3. A Lonely Man

I had a lousy war. After the disaster my life had become, I thought I'd found my purpose. A career in service to comrades and country. An ambush in my second tour nearly killed me; the four-month infection ended my career.

So much for *belonging*.

Discharged, I limped back to England with nowhere to go: parents dead, brother estranged, Alice and Mary, gone.

I did what any unhappy man would in my position: lived too large on limited resources, pretending everything was fine.

Nothing is as lonely as being lonely in London, with no friends, no prospects, no money and no hope.

Then Tom Stamford, a fellow St Bart's graduate, found me loitering over a pint at the Criterion.

"You look terrible," he said, "Have lunch with me—I hate eating alone—and tell me all!"

I'd intended to stand on my pride, but Tom's face invites confession, and so I confessed.

"I know a chap who needs a flatmate," Tom replied. "He's odd, but I recall you like odd."

I'd let that show?

So I met Sherlock Holmes: eccentric, grey-eyed bachelor of unusual intellect and beautiful hands. Sherlock read my Afghanistan history in one unjudgemental glance. I could have kissed him.

Later, in thanks, I kissed Tom instead.

But I might kiss Sherlock yet, if I ever again feel brave.

4. Unwelcome

221B Baker Street wasn't the most restful residence for a war veteran, but it suited John Watson down to the bone. He was supposed to be recuperating that February, but idleness imposed rather than indolence by choice was galling.

Fortunately, Sherlock Holmes was a private consulting detective who filled the sitting room with an endless parade of fascinating individuals seeking advice. Many arrived stricken with anxiety and left with lighter hearts.

On Day Four of cohabitation, John was called on to administer first aid to a high-strung headmaster who fainted on the rug. Sherlock promptly invited John to sit in on consultations and provide medical opinions.

John listened, observed, felt useful again. When not diagnosing, he watched Sherlock work and quietly sketched portraits of the striking cheekbones, eyes, hands, belonging to his flatmate.

He looks kissable, John thought wistfully.

Day Seven brought him up short. An excitable and grateful young client grasped Sherlock's hands and kissed his cheek. Sherlock froze, withdrew. The speed with which he made space between them was declaration enough, but he added after the client left: "I hate when they do that." He swabbed the offended cheek with his sleeve.

"A bit forward," agreed John.

"I dislike being touched," said Sherlock with an uneasy frown.

Note to self, realised John ruefully. *Kissing Sherlock is out of bounds.*

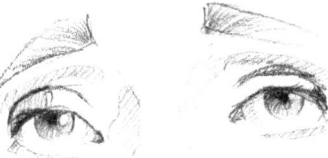

5. Glasgow Kiss

14 February
- place Davidoff order—further 20 tobacco types
- slides (ash samples)
- flame-retardant gloves
- research: removing scorch marks from laminate
- research: cost of replacing laminate benchtops w. granite/stainless steel

Dr W. proving an excellent housemate. Decision to inc. him on consultations effective. Less fidgety with something to do. Offers sensible medical insights. Bedside manner A+ (Headmaster Huxtable rates him, anyway.) His presence reassuring to anxious clients. Good face: friendly. Looks reliable. Handsome, which doesn't hurt. Military bearing just quelling enough; doc demeanour just reassuring enough. Scribbles in notebook, which looks studious.

Note: not writing. Sketching? Doodles? Former, I expect. Purposeful.

Note: Sketches of the clients? What catches his attention? Set up mirror over mantel to reflect his notebook.

15 February
JW is delightful. That brute Roylott showed up for a pound of flesh now the Stoner heiress knows his game. R. came at me with the poker. J, despite that stiff shoulder, was straight in there, uppercut like Sam Merton. Beautiful to see: combination of decisiveness, grace, speed & ruthlessness. Pity Roylott's head is so hard. Bastard swung at me again. J grabbed his coat to swing him off balance; head-butted right in the bridge of the nose. Perfect Glasgow Kiss. Blood everywhere, all Roylott's. J patched him up & stood guard till Lestrade arrived.

Finally, a flatmate I can bear.

6. Buried Treasure

Olivier Dunedin came to Sherlock Holmes in great agitation, wondering if his Aunt Lacey's estate consisted of more than the contents of her shabby council flat, a pet, and a rusty 1996 Mini Cooper.

"She'd started joking she had buried treasure for me," Dunedin said to the detective. In another chair, Dr Watson doodled, made notes. "She'd go prospecting with a metal detector on weekends, around Kent and Sussex."

"Perhaps it *was* a joke," suggested Holmes

"Perhaps, but this was with her will." Dunedin produced a map, hand-drawn on thick, wrinkled paper, depicting an island, a shipwreck, a skeleton, a shoal of fish and an overflowing treasure chest.

Holmes examined it; ran his fingers over front and back; even sniffed it. "Dr Watson?"

The Doctor made his own examination. "Smells funny. Ammonia. It's stained and wrinkled, like it's been wet. It's hardly an antique."

Holmes beamed at him. To Dunedin he said, "Did your aunt keep an aquarium?"

"Yes."

"Come, John!"

At the council house in Banstead, Dunedin showed them the aquarium containing its large, lone goldfish, Caesar. With a grin, the detective rolled up his sleeve, reached gently into the piratically decorated tank—Caesar sucked fish-kisses on his forearm—and withdrew a closed plastic chest.

Inside it was the remarkable treasure Aunt Lacey had unearthed: a priceless, gem-encrusted Roman bracelet.

7. Landlady

Across their adjoining, flower-bedecked fence, Maria Turner invited Ellie Hudson over for an afternoon tipple.

"How are the new tenants, El?" Maria handed Ellie a glass of chardonnay.

Ellie, never impulsive, considered as she sipped.

"Mr Holmes is unpredictable," she said at last, "He works from home; people are there all hours. He fancies himself a chemist, and a violinist. I like him, even if he burned the kitchen bench. The doctor's more of a puzzle. The police nicked a violent client; he left with a bloody nose. Dr Watson strutted about after with a goose-egg on his forehead and a Cheshire-cat grin."

"Worrying."

"Not really, but he's restless. He paces a lot. Scared the life out of me to hear someone in the garden in the wee hours, until I realised it was him."

"Why was he skulking around at arse o'clock?"

"Sketching by streetlight, oddly enough. I suppose he couldn't sleep. Jumped like a jackrabbit when I said hello, poor beggar. Everything went flying. Army veteran, you know."

"Don't sneak up on him, then. My sister still gets the shakes."

"Don't you start. Mr Holmes gave me the same lecture. Like he's afraid I'll scare the doctor off."

"Well if they give you trouble, I'll give back twice as much." Maria kissed Ellie's fingers. "Nobody messes with my baby."

8. Flora and Fauna

"Sherlock, don't touch it!"

"Gloves, John, see? I don't know where you get this impression I'm so careless."

"The kitchen bench you scorched has something to do with it. Why is Ellie growing monkshood?"

"It's common enough. Poisoning is rare: it tastes disgusting."

"Didn't stop my dog Major accidentally eating it and dropping dead when I was ten. Awful stuff. Why are you picking it?"

"I keep pressings of London's common toxic plants. Hold that specimen bag open for me? Flower, stem, leaf, root. Perfect."

"Is this the new version of your 'name that tobacco ash' journal?"

"Sod off. Ah! Kiss me over the garden gate."

"Beg pardon?"

"Botany, John. *Persicaria orientalis.* That tall red plant growing at the fence."

"Oh."

"Are you all right?"

"Yep. Fine. Just fine. Is that toxic too?"

"No, just tall. Oh, what's this among the phlox? That's an excellent sketch of a cat..."

"Give it here. *Now!* Sorry. Ah. Sorry. It's private."

"That's the notebook you doodle in when we interview clients."

"Yeah."

"You dropped it here last night. You couldn't sleep. Our landlady startled you."

"How did you know? Never mind. Who's in a garden at bloody 3am anyway?"

"Apart from you and the cat? Ellie returning from a tryst with her boyfriend."

"Doesn't she have a girlfriend?"

"No reason she can't have both."

9. The Mystery of the Steampunk Jeweller

I've had the most interesting three weeks of my life: including my years in the army. Baker Street's also free of friendly fire, unless you count the times Sherlock's chemistry experiments become alarming.

Besides Sherlock and experiments, his clients are fascinating. Two days ago, Henrietta Ravensdale (her pseudonym) came to consult Sherlock.

He asked me to sit in. He says my drawings are illuminating, whatever *that* means. (I sketch clients during interviews now, since I caught him peeking in the mantel mirror. Less weird if they're not just him.)

Ravensdale wore mostly brown. Steampunk fashion, apparently. Also gold pince-nez and jewellery crafted from cogs, brass, and crystal. One brooch, bronze filigree framing a tiny screen, displayed a looping animation of two robots kissing.

Sherlock began by demonstrating he's not the run-of-the-mill P.I. (He gives me such a look when I call him that. Those eyes of his! I shouldn't tease.)

"Train driver by profession; jeweller by vocation," he said before she spoke, "Trading up from hobbyist to entrepreneur. Once owned a cat, but no longer. Single…"

Ravensdale raised an uncowed brow. "You think I'm wasting your time on a phantasm," she said. "The police were the same. That doesn't keep this from buzzing when it shouldn't."

In her palm was an exquisite brooch made of gears and amber: a clockwork bee.

10. An Unexplained Buzzing

Sherlock's eyes lit up at the clockwork bee. He sat eagerly forward to peer at it. (My fingers itched to sketch his parted lips as he drew in an animated breath.)

Stripes of amber and black tungsten combined with cogs, springs, wires, hands and tiny clock parts I couldn't name, to form a delicate, stunning work of wearable art.

His fingers twitched. "May I?"

Henrietta Ravensdale nodded.

Sherlock took it carefully from her palm and examined it with the antique jeweller's loupe he keeps in his breast pocket. She regarded the brass and nacre loupe as avidly as I watched him turning the bee in his long, mobile fingers. He exclaimed when he saw its underside, then wound the small serrated crown there. The bee's wings, head and antennae moved, kissing Sherlock's fingers with its motion.

Lucky bee.

"Ingenious! But what's the problem?"

"Sometimes it buzzes." At his frown, Ravensdale added, "I didn't design it to buzz."

I was puzzled. "It's not buzzing now."

"No. It only happens at home. Only sometimes."

"When?" Sherlock asked. "For how long?"

"During the last week. In the evening mostly."

"That's no reason to consult the police as you did, or me."

"It scares me," she confessed, pale.

"Why?"

"I don't know."

"Let's investigate *in situ*," Sherlock offered. "You'll come, John?"

I grinned. "You bet."

11. The Waggle Dance

Sherlock learned the clockwork bee's history on the journey to Ravensdale's apartment in North Harrow.

"I've used clock and watch parts," said Henrietta. "The winding mechanisms make it move. It's very fine work. I'll never sell it for anything like it cost me in craft hours. I wanted to make them commercially, using my blueprints, but Stephan said it wasn't viable."

"Who's he?" I asked.

"From work. He's into steampunk too."

"Expert, is he?" Sherlock asked.

"He had a friend who knew a friend. He showed the guy my prototype, but brought it back last week saying it was a no-go."

On Whittington Way, Henrietta used an electronic key to open her garage, below the apartments. "I use it as a workroom. Metalwork stinks up the apartment too much. Here they are!" She drew out a roll of papers, kissing the blueprints like she was relieved to see them. "My life's work!" she joked nervously.

Sherlock's expression was keen, almost elated, which meant he was putting together facts which I didn't even know existed yet. I can do that with a patient's lifestyle and symptoms. He can do it with everything else.

"Your bee's waggle dance began after he returned it to you?"

"Yes. But—waggle dance?"

"A form of communication between honeybees," said Sherlock. "I know what's happening, I believe."

12. Antennae

Sherlock hates to explain when he can demonstrate, which is why we were all waiting in the shadows of Henrietta's closed workroom as night fell.

At 7pm, the clockwork bee in his palm buzzed—a short, sharp hum, legs and antennae dancing with the vibration. Sherlock grinned and pressed it under his chin.

The door of the garage opened, unbidden, in front of us. A man stood there, a remote control in his hand.

"Stephan!" Henrietta cried.

Stephan bolted but didn't get far with his collar in my fist. He kicked. I knocked his feet out from under him. He kissed dirt.

"Your would-be thief." Sherlock beamed at Henrietta. At *me*. "Your manufacturing plans *are* viable. Potentially lucrative. Stephan returned the prototype with an addition—an electronic device to open your garage so he could steal the blueprints. However, the signal was too weak for his remote to work. He miscalculated."

"You used your body to boost the signal! Clever!" I applauded.

"How did you know?" asked Henrietta.

"The buzz frightened you. You were so relieved to find your blueprints you kissed them. Instinctively you knew they were at risk. Put this against Stephan's brief possession of the bee and the after-hours activity, *voila*, his plot was revealed."

Henrietta rewarded Sherlock with the first bee made by her business, Waggle Bots.

13. Tell Me More

Tom Stamford	John Watson
All ok there? Or should I be looking for a new place for you?	
	Everything great. Why wouldn't it be?
Sherlock's not everyone's cup of tea.	
	Why introduce us then?
Neither are you! ☺	
	Behold my hysterical laughter face, Tom. ☺ That's how funny you are.
He's got odd hobbies I know. Bit disruptive. Getting your rest? You're supposed to be on R&R.	
	It's not a hobby. It's his job.
What is?	
	Private eye. ☺ Consulting detective actually. Only call him a PI cos he pouts prettily when I do.
A pretty pouter, eh? You little devil. Three Continents Watson strikes again!	
	It's not like that. We're mates.
Say that again without blushing.	
	:-P
All the nice boys love a soldier Johnny!	

Ah.

FFS, no. Just friends, like I said.

Ah what?

Just ah.
So what have you and your just a friend been up to?
Johnny?
John?
John?
I'm just kidding. Don't sulk.

Not sulking you twat. Sherlock's explaining waggle dances.

Sounds like some new kind of euphemism.

Stop being a muppet.

Fine. All good then?

Great, like I said. He's taken me on a few cases. Fascinating stuff.

Is this what recuperation looks like to you?

Yes, smartarse.

As long as you're happy. XXX

I am. Bloody happy. Thanks for the intro.

My pleasure, bruh.

17

14. No Limits

27 February
JW's limits

Physically solid (matches personality). ~~Sun-kissed.~~ Tanned. Ordinarily robust; vigour returning.

Divorced. ~~Bi?~~

In own field, JW v. observant. Often confirms my views or has insights on cases. However, seems unable to link wider ideas unrelated to diagnosis. Can't fault him for that. Not many can.

Gullible? Believes my exhaustive descriptions of where I received mud splashes during my walks. My knowledge is A+, but I cheat. (I know where I went.) Humouring me? Playing along with the joke? So inscrutable sometimes.

Fights with surgical effectiveness. Fewest blows for greatest result. Improved health helps. Always been ready to commit to a fight—quelling Stephan. Uppercut to Roylott! ~~Thrilling!~~

Medical knowledge: excellent doctor. Professional interest in traumatic injury. Subscribes *Lancet*, other med. journals. Competent hands, excellent manner. He'll be wasted as a GP.

Has a pleasant tenor. Sings with the radio when thinks he's alone. Enjoys my violin, when I'm bothering with an actual piece. Note: learn some popular pieces; see if he'll sing along.

Fine anatomical & portrait artist.

What else? Patient. Well read. Brave. ~~Handsome.~~ Confident; not arrogant. Appreciates the outré & relief from humdrum. Increasingly indispensable. Will I ever get his limits?

J listens where I declaim. Steady where I'm moody. Calm where I'm intense.

Works well with me. *Laughs* with me.

J gives me *balance.*

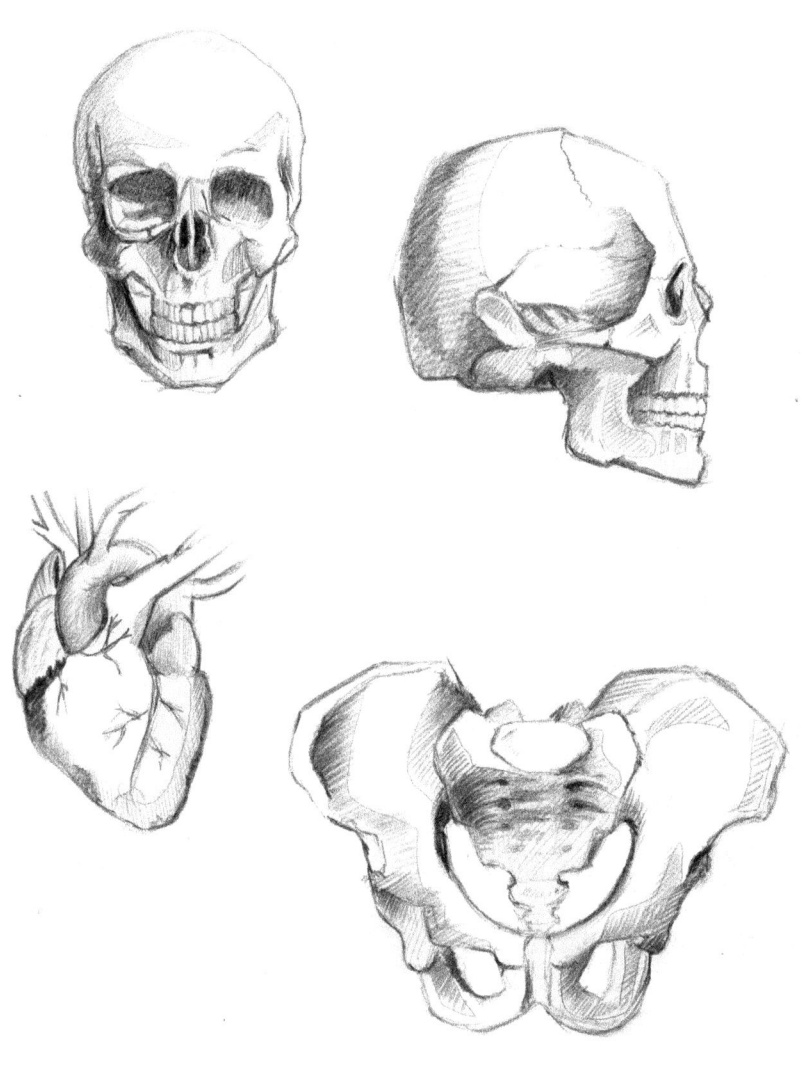

15. Person or Persons Unknown

Sherlock was in a mood, playing his violin like he meant it harm. His temper's foul when he's without work for more than a week.

I knew blokes in Helmand who got antsy between patrols. Not boredom, exactly. More a sense of looming threat, so they wanted to act, not fret. I don't know why not working makes Sherlock fret, but I don't take it personally. The noise is awful, though.

I thought I was hiding how the violin torture made my teeth hurt, but he looked at me and launched into Paganini's *Caprice 24* (that's what he says it's called). He smiles when he plays it, eyes closed, dreamy expression. Stupid me wanted to kiss that smile right into me.

I was surreptitiously trying to capture the grace of his hand on the bow when a client knocked. I hid the sketchbook and opened the door.

The client, a tall woman, had to speak over Paganini. "I have an urgent case."

Sherlock stopped mid-phrase, expression transformed from dreamy to eager in an instant.

"Inspector Lestrade! Speak! Don't mind Doctor Watson. He assists me. That is, John, would you like to assist me?"

"If I can."

Unconvinced, Inspector Lestrade frowned.

"John has invaluable medical expertise," Sherlock explained. "Your case?"

"We have a letter threatening murder. Two suspects. As yet, no body."

16. Observations of a D.I.

Holmes was at his violin as I arrived. It indicated a good mood—he attacks it like a brute when he's bored. Door opened by the flatmate he'd talked about. (This Watson tried to hide a notebook behind his back. Had sketches of hands in it. Odd thing to hide.)

Gave Holmes the case outline.

Constables Franklin and Ricci, on their morning beat, overheard a woman yelling abuse. Found suspect, Alexis Gorski, 14 Brownlow Mews, Clerkenwell, screaming threats through the letterbox of no. 16 at 9:30am. When asked to settle down, Gorski punched Franklin in the face, and was then apprehended by Ricci.

Occupant of 16, Miriam Somerset, reported she threw Gorski out after words exchanged about Gorski's cat using Somerset's garden as a litter tray.

Neighbours confirm and further advise they are former lovers; took one month to go from kissing to verbal abuse, property destruction, vandalism.

Cat's missing. This morning, peace talks over herbal tea became death threats.

Showed Holmes the letter we found under the threshold of 16 after we spoke to Somerset. Somerset and Gorski both being questioned: neither will admit to writing the letter.

Holmes took one look, told Doc Watson to bring his kit, and me to call an ambulance, then off we dashed.

The letter says:

I'll KILL YOU. YOU ARE ALREADY DEAD. BITCH.

17. Friend and Colleague

The letter wasn't only a threat: it was a confession. YOU ARE ALREADY DEAD. But who had poisoned whom? And why wouldn't its recipient accuse the other of writing it?

Sherlock knew of only one scenario to explain it.

The ambulance was taking Miriam Somerset away when they arrived.

Lestrade thought it was Case Solved. Sherlock knew better, shouting for medical access to the second prisoner. John had no more clues than Lestrade (and no fewer) but unlike Lestrade, he readily echoed Sherlock's urgency. "Ms Gorski needs medical attention immediately!" he insisted, with a commanding snap.

John's brisk authority stirred Sherlock's blood. Even Lestrade responded with alacrity. "Let him through!"

Just in time: John administered the kiss of life to Gorski while another ambulance was despatched.

Afterwards, Sherlock proudly introduced John to the Met as "my friend and colleague Dr Watson".

The solution? Gorski and Somerset were simultaneous murderers and victims combined. Toxicology tests later showed that Somerset made poisoned tea from oleander; while Gorski put digitalis in Somerset's coffee.

Sherlock explained.

"Gorski wrote the letter, so naturally said nothing. However, Somerset, unaware she'd also been poisoned, didn't accuse Gorski because of a guilty conscience. She irrationally feared discovery if she spoke up."

At least the cat had a happy ending: Somerset had given it to the cats' home at Battersea.

18. Comfort Food

A driver was waiting when Seb left behind the six months of stinking cell, stupid cellmate, terrible food and brutal hierarchy.

Doing time had its dangers, but Cairy, who'd promised to shank Seb and his cellmate, was himself shanked two days later. Nothing directly to do with Seb of course. But Seb had people on the outside looking out for him on the inside.

Seb got into the passenger seat. He could smell the comforting nutmeg and cinnamon, the raisins. It made his mouth water.

The driver, a paper bag on his lap, regarded him critically; with concern.

"You've lost weight."

"Yeah."

"Look fit, though."

"Killed a bit of time throwing weights about. Six months is no joke, even on purpose."

"Did he talk?"

"Feck, yeah. I was his best mate, wasn't I, after I took credit for Cairy. Nice work that, Liam."

"James arranged for Cairy."

"Professor Fecking Organised." Seb's admiration was grudging, as always.

"So?"

"Prescott said where he hid it. Some poxy war veteran's living on top of it now, though."

"James'll come up with something."

"Course he will, Liam"

"Here." Liam gave him the bag.

Seb plucked out the contents and kissed the foil. Unwrapping it, he let the scent of spiced, sweet bun and good Irish butter waft up. His traditional release-day treat. Mam's home-made barmbrack.

19. Last Post

Arriving home, Sherlock saw the pocket watch and, assuming a client had left it, examined it with his loupe.

A late Victorian antique, he surmised from the casing.

John stood over the kettle, back to the table, stance rigid. Shoulder aching? Poor sleep? Sherlock decided deduction could serve as distraction.

"A valuable family heirloom," he said, "Maintained beautifully for several generations but fell into the hands of a slovenly heir. From these scratches and dents, an alcoholic or addict. The marks aren't recent. Likely deceased…"

He flicked the casing open.

"Stop."

John's grim, red-rimmed gaze halted him. Sherlock perceived now the letter crushed in John's grip. The case open, he glanced down to see H.W. engraved inside.

"Ah. Not a client. Yours. No. Your…father's?"

"Then Hugh's. Now mine. It took them months to find me." John's fist tightened on the crushed letter. "They tried the army, the hospital, rehab, the bedsit, now here. Hugh's been dead for months and I didn't know."

"John, I'm…"

"Overdose. I always expected it. We haven't spoken in years. I told him. Last time he stole from me, before I was deployed. I've had enough. I can't save you. My last words to him were the kiss-off."

"I'm sorry. For. Your loss. For. This. I didn't realise…"

"You're not omniscient then."

"No."

John nodded once. Brusquely.

20. Debrief

Violet "Blue" Murray	John Watson
Missed you last night!	
	Sthg came up. Next time.
K-Jam got ratfaced and sang showtunes. ☺	
	O_o
Seriously tho. U ok? I heard about Hugh. I'm sorry. I know things weren't good between you.	
	Yeah.
You couldn't have helped him.	
	I'll never know now. I stopped trying.
Not your fault. He stole your dad's watch. Your savings. He screwed your wife. Used up all his chances.	
	I really spilled my guts while you were patching me up out there.
Good distraction from all the bleeding. Fuckers got no respect for a medical convoy.	
	I remember.
Fuck. Sorry. ☹ My bedside manner's still awesome.	
	Sorry, Blue. Cranky bugger today. Flatmate touched a nerve.

Your Detective?	
	He found the watch but not the letter. Deduced all about Hugh from it. Bit close to the bone.
You said he was a smartarse.	
	I said he was *clever*.
You love smartarses tho. You gushed about this one last drinks.	
	I didn't gush.
You keep telling yourself that.	
	:-p I overreacted.
Went for one of your long cranky walks?	
	Yeah.
Feel better?	
	A bit. And Sherlock apologised.
Not a total twat.	
	He's not a twat.
Gushing again.	
	Fuck you.
:-*	
	You only get away with this shit cos I owe you my life.
And I'm funny.	
	Keep telling yourself that, Blue.

21. Regrets, I Have a Few

10 March
To do:
  - *make it up to J*
  - *cease being a self-absorbed twat*

I meant to distract him. *Impress* him. I misread his posture & all I've done is give him grief. Forget that though he's easy to read (generally) he keeps his history well-guarded. Lack data. Make stupid mistakes.

He left angry, returned as calm as ever. We pretend it never happened. He has put the watch away (from me). Locked in his army trunk, I assume. With other secrets?

Fully understand his reaction now, when he saw the track scars on my arm at Dunedin's fish tank. I wondered at the lack of lecture with underlying gloom. Not mere doctorly disapproval. I knew his medical experience wasn't all shrapnel and VD. He knew what the scars were; knew they were old.

I didn't know they matched his brother's.

Hugh's scars were clearly never *old*. Will mine always be? I keep the syringe, fresh needle, a hit. In case. Haven't needed one for so long, but cannot promise that will always be so. Will not lie to myself about it.

~~I wanted to kiss his brow & never make him frown again.~~
~~Stupid to think I could achieve that.~~

I boast my superior intelligence, but my feet are made of clay, like any man. Nevertheless. I can do better.

22. Amends

"What's this?"

"Isn't it obvious, John?"

"It's a very handsome pocket moleskin sketchbook. It's much too fine for my scribbles."

"Your studies are perfectly well-rendered."

"Oh. You've…seen them."

"Some. You've a gift for depicting our clients' notable features. Roylott's scowl; Dunedin's ears; Ravensdale's bee. I imagine your draughtsmanship was honed at medical school."

"Back then it was internal organs. I developed the habit of sketching individual features in Afghanistan. Easy to abandon in an emergency."

"Of which there were many."

"A good number, yeah. Hey, you've inscribed it... is this a…kiss? Sherlock?"

"No! Ah. Not a kiss. The pen slipped."

"Just teasing. Thank you. It's very kind."

"Not kind. Warranted."

"You weren't to know about Hugh."

"Observation and deducing from what I observe is meant to be my particular skill, John. I not only failed to observe, I caused you distress with my insensitivity. I really am terribly sorry."

"I shouldn't have snapped at you."

"Why not? You tolerate a good deal as my flatmate, John. The occasional snap is forgivable, especially under the circumstances."

"You're not at all difficult to live with, you know. I like it here. I like living with you, Sherlock. Going on cases with you."

"Good. I like you too. Living with you. Too. Is that the time? I must dash."

"Right now? Oh…ah. Okay. Bye."

23. A Dream to Build a Kiss On

For the trained reasoner, Sherlock Holmes had proclaimed, the softer passions were grit in the logic machine, a crack in the lens of observation.

Accounting for strong emotions—such powerful motivators—was essential in the field of deduction. But! The mind of the reasoner must remain unclouded! All emotions, most especially *love*, were not for him.

(He'd made that grave error once. *Never again*, he'd sworn.)

What a fatuous git he was, to think pretending not to feel was the same as not feeling.

Because he was *aflame*, less than two months into their…was it a friendship? In 38 days, Dr Watson had become Sherlock's intriguing flatmate; a valued medical consultant; a welcome comrade-in-arms; and the object of Sherlock's repressed desires.

The subconscious X in the sketchbook inscription was clue enough. Those crossed-out words in his diary, as though obliteration made them un-thought.

But today Sherlock woke with hot skin, shaft erect, tip wet, body arching towards the dream of John Watson, who'd moments before been kissing him.

Such a voluptuous reaction to such a chaste, imaginary kiss. Warm lips on his: full of care, devotion, passion.

That kiss, bestowed so easily in a dream, was impossible by daylight. Sherlock Holmes wasn't that kind of man. He had made that emphatically so himself.

What, Sherlock thought bitterly, a load of *bollocks*.

24. Lust is Not the Problem

Lust, he could have managed. John Watson knew lust. His fancy had been excited by all manner of charms. Delightful combinations of a strong arm and a knowing eye; a plush lower lip and stubbled jaw; a clever wit and an earthy laugh; the curve of a well-made arse and the swell of reciprocal arousal.

Physical attraction came and went, in raucous, joyful one night stands, or over several days of what-the-hell. Lust was not John Watson's problem. Lust could be despatched. One quick wank or a long, slow pull, savouring the temptation of cannot-be in solitary fantasy.

However, the stuttering of his heart when Sherlock Holmes shone light on other people's darkness was another matter entirely. John's pulse fluttered like an overwrought teen at the sound of Sherlock's voice, at the flash of inspiration and eager intelligence in piercing grey eyes. Sherlock's rare smiles, especially when John had been the cause, lit up the sky of John's heart.

In Sherlock's presence, the long and weary months of pain and loss evaporated into mist, leaving John game for any task, if Sherlock asked it of him.

John had kissed a hundred lovers from London to Kandahar to Montreal. He'd never yearned so helplessly to kiss one beautiful, slender wrist.

He lusted, yes. But this was love—a much more dangerous business.

25. Big Brother

My brother is a fine man: brilliant, passionate, though prone to bursts of unseemly energy. He visited in one such burst today. I understand Sherlock's need for activity, even if I don't share it, so I sent him to find Mr Melas, our Greek interpreter.

Sherlock enterprisingly picked the lock of Melas' flat and concluded—from racing guides, the lack of pawnable electronics, and numbers scrawled on an envelope—that gambling debts drove Melas into hiding at Gravesend. I despatched a deputy to retrieve him.

Sherlock took tea with me in Pall Mall. He wasn't himself.

"You have feelings for your flatmate," I said (putting two and two and two together).

"No!" Then, resigned, "I'm not the falling-in-love kind."

"Yet, you have."

"Yes."

"Reciprocated?"

"He's…interested."

"But?"

"I don't do relationships."

"You told him this?"

Sherlock's truculent-rueful expression answered.

"Might you reverse that policy?"

"I instigated it for a *reason*."

"The past is *past*, Sherlock."

"Yet my limitations remain. What if John gets bored?"

Some days, I'd happily stir myself to properly thrash Reginald Musgrave.

"Dr Watson's a veteran. Surely you're at least as interesting as a war."

"When I'm working, yes."
Alas, his bruised heart. "Not everyone's cruel."
"John's kind," he conceded.
I kissed Sherlock's cheek in farewell. He left happier.
Perhaps Sherlock's not, after all, destined to be a bachelor.

26. Windswept

John drew in his old sketchbook, recalling from mind to fingertips the shape of Sherlock's sharp-eyed gaze. Fine brows drawn down, dark lashes pronounced against pale skin, eyes alive with fascination as he examined a letter.

He really had to stop drawing his flatmate in such intimate detail. If Sherlock ever actually found this sketchbook, the game would be up entirely.

Hearing Sherlock ascending the stairs, John shoved the book under his shirt. He seized the new one, containing less incriminating art.

Sherlock's hair was tousled, cheeks flushed with fresh air.

Oh, to make him windswept from kissing!

"Busy morning?" John asked, his voice admirably steady.

"I visited my brother."

"You have a brother?"

"Mycroft. He's older, and much smarter, but lazy as a cat in a sunbeam. I investigate things for him when he won't drag himself out of doors. Today it was a missing man."

"Did you find him?"

"He was hiding in Gravesend. Mycroft could've deduced it himself, if he'd gone to Melas' house as I did. It's not much good having art in the blood if you don't exercise it. Speaking of which, you've been drawing today."

John showed him the girl he'd drawn from memory that morning. (His lost Alice.)

His other love letters in line art were tucked safely away, beside his heart's steady beat.

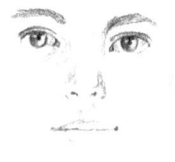

34

27. The Right Thing to Do

Mary had been John's friend since before their GCSEs. The pregnancy changed all their plans. At 19, he'd done the Right Thing.

They'd lived with his father while John studied. Mary had Alice. They were happy-ish.

Then Hugh came home.

John didn't blame Mary for the affair. Despite trying, he wasn't much of a husband. John loved Mary; but he wasn't *in* love.

But to catch her kissing *Hugh?*

John did the Right Thing. He gave Mary her divorce.

Betrayed, John ran towards service, transferring to an RAMC medical cadetship. He served at Frimley Park MoD hospital; graduated Sandhurst; joined the Colchester regiment.

Hugh had wasted no time hurting Mary and five-year-old Alice too. Unredeemed (irredeemable) he'd vanished with their savings.

John still tried to help Hugh. The Right Thing. Then Hugh stole again; hocked the family heirlooms.

"Enough," John told Hugh. "I can't help you. Won't."

John transferred to a medical evacuation unit; went to Afghanistan where he *could* help.

Where he nearly died.

John clawed back to life through emergency then reconstructive surgery; near-fatal fever; medical discharge. Alone, lonely, useless, until Tom introduced him to Sherlock.

John loved his unexpected, exciting new life. He loved his friend. He didn't care if it was the Right Thing to Do anymore. He *loved* him.

Even if Sherlock didn't love him back.

28. M.I.A.

John kissed Blue hello and offered her a seat. Instead, Blue Murray restlessly paced the hearthrug.

"Here," gestured John. His chair faced the room, back to the wall, away from the window.

His friend visibly relaxed as she sat.

"When did you last see Sergeant Jambur?" prompted Sherlock.

"He got squiffy at drinks and sang showtunes. Like he does, eh Trixie?

"And how," John agreed.

"They're saying he offed himself," said Blue, "But he wouldn't."

Sherlock ignored the 'Trixie'. (Army nickname: relating to …Trixie Belden?) "Jambur's wheelchair was found by the river yesterday."

Anger flashed. "He *wouldn't*."

Suicide rates among veterans were distressingly high, as John and Murray knew. *Are you sure?* Unsaid.

Sherlock glanced at John's grim expression and didn't argue. (*Do better.*)

"Your thoughts, John?"

"I wouldn't have called Kris high risk. Blue and I know the stats. We were friends with some of them. K-Jam had adjusted well."

"I'm a likelier candidate," grumbled Blue, tucked into John's chair, eyes on all potential exits. Sherlock didn't doubt it.

"Has anything changed about him lately?"

"He'd moved to a new flat," said John. "Tiny place."

"Says he's being stalked by redheads. On the tube; at the off-licence; selling the Big Issue."

Sherlock rose, intrigued and brisk. "Get your coats," he said, doing the same, "I want to see his bedsit."

29. The Pawnbroker's Holiday

K-Jam's place was a granny flat in Hackney. His landlord, Jay Wilson, pawnbroker by trade, had just returned from a disappointing holiday.

"It was meant to be *Brighton*. Lewes isn't Brighton. Nowhere near the sea! The castle's fine I suppose, but I wanted sea breezes. The Air BNB flat was nasty. The owners hadn't even cleaned. I wouldn't have stayed the whole ten days except I won the trip."

Sherlock was alert. "Won it? How?"

"Some charity or league. I don't remember buying tickets, but only an idiot ignores the kiss of luck, eh?"

Sherlock refrained from so labelling idiots who took unexplained windfalls at face value.

"You left a stranger alone here?"

"I have the house keys. It's not like Jambur can get up the stairs to break in. Anyway, I took him on in part to keep watch in my absence. A month paid in advance, and now he's done a bunk. Some of these ex-army blokes are terribly unreliable."

John and Blue bristled. Wilson was oblivious.

Sherlock circumvented their offended snarling. "When did Jambur move in?"

"The day before I left for Brighton. Well. *Lewes*."

"Can we see his room?"

"Owes you money, eh? I'll get the key."

The door opened on wild disarray: everything flung to the edges of the dismal lodgings, like Jambur had been burgled.

30. Kryptonite

Trixie, Holmes and I went to the River Lee where K-Jam's wheelchair was found near a broken-down landing-stage.

John's smug crush was grinning. I honestly don't know what Trixie sees in him. So he's handsome, clever and a smartarse. Trixie's Kryptonite. Still.

"Why are you grinning?" I was annoyed.

"Jambur's flat wasn't randomly burgled. Everything was pushed away from the centre. The floorboards were loose. The intruder found what they were after."

"How does that fucking help?"

"Blue, be fair, Sherlock's just started…" John, leaping to his crush's defence.

"It helps because you're right. Jambur didn't commit suicide. He was forcibly removed. Did you see the fingernail marks on the door jamb? Blood drops in the sink, too far back for Jambur to reach. He fought them. Two redheads, by the hairs. Dark, curly hair was more plentiful. Jambur's, yes?"

"Yes."

"I believe your friend is still alive."

"Don't lie to me. They've killed him." So I was bitter. Fucking sue me.

"They've tried," Holmes said, examining the banks, "But your friend can swim."

John looked at Holmes like he was made of songbirds. "Kris swims for therapy. Did he dive in?"

"Pushed, but see? Someone sheltered under the jetty. There's fresh marks in the wood. No emerging marks near. He escaped."

I was so relieved, I kissed the smug bastard.

31. Follow the Leader

Sherlock placed fingertips to cheek, where Blue had kissed him.

"Premature," he said, "We haven't found Jambur yet."

"You will," asserted John.

John's confidence was galvanising. Sherlock examined the jetty ruins and the Lee for day-old clues. He peered across the river to the marshes; the boats moored along the banks.

He flashed a grin at John, whipped off coat and shoes, dived into the river.

"Sherlock!" John began stripping off.

"What the fuck?" cursed Blue.

John, barefoot, waded in. "If K-Jam could swim it, we can."

"There's a fucking bridge!" Blue yelled, but he was gone.

Carrying their gear, Blue finally joined the wet pair on the towpath. John had put a blanket around Kris Jambur's shoulders.

"T-t-t-took th' long way, Blue?" K-Jam grinned through his chattering teeth. Blue dropped to her knees to hug him. Kiss his brow.

"Thank God," she whispered. "Thank God."

"Sherlock realised Kris hadn't come out on the jetty side," praised John, "Then he saw this boat: low sides, climbable. Moored for weeks, judging by the algae on the bow. Scraped algae, and movement belowdecks."

"So Sherlock swam the Lee fully dressed? And you followed? Jesus, Trix, you got it bad."

Jambur laughed wheezily. Sherlock and John didn't look at each other.

"What the fuck happened to you, K-Jam?" Blue asked.

"T-two arseholes from B-belfast."

32. Seb and Liam

Ellie Hudson brought hot tea to Sherlock's damp friends as they waited for Lestrade, partly because they'd invaded her kitchen and partly to glean details to share with Maria.

Sherlock, animated, was showing off for his doctor.

"Clearly these redheads needed unobserved access to the flat, to extract whatever was hidden there. They contrived to remove Wilson with a simple con, but you were more stubborn."

"I'd just moved in, and don't like being out much."

Blue squeezed Kris' hand. He lifted their entwined fingers to kiss her knuckles.

"They shadowed you. When you wouldn't stay away long enough, they took more direct action."

"They hit me on the fucking head."

"They tried to kill him." Blue's grim expression promised retribution.

"They were sloppy. They assumed because Kris can't walk, he couldn't swim. Luckily, the cold water revived him."

"They had Irish accents. Seb and Liam. They'd banged up my chair, the sods. If I'd pulled myself ashore there and they came back, I wouldn't have got far. Then I saw the boats opposite and figured I'd climb up the ropes and hide on board till someone found me."

"What now?" Blue asked.

"We find out who Seb and Liam are," said John.

"It'll take time," advised Sherlock.

"But you will," John asserted warmly. "You're clever, and stubborn as a bull."

33. BlueJam

Two hours later, Kris Jambur, in a wheelchair John had arranged, watched Blue tidy his flat.

"Your lucky army mug is still intact."

"Blue."

"Still gonna kick their bollocks through their oesophagus."

"Blue?"

"Yeah?"

"You reckon Trixie and his detective'll sort themselves out?"

Blue laughed. "Trixie's practically flashing a 'Shag me!' beacon."

"Sherlock preens like rooster if John even *looks* at him."

"A right cock."

"Don't you like him?"

Blue stacked magazines on the floor. "He's okay. If he breaks John's heart I'll smack him."

"What about mine, then?"

"What?"

"*My* heart."

Blue stared, rabbit in the headlights.

"When are we going to do something about us, Blue?" Kris wrestled his unfamiliar chair closer to her and sent the magazines flying. He cursed, tried again, banged into the coffee table then stopped, defeated.

"I'm a mess, K-Jam. Anti-anxiety meds, nightmares. My hands still reek of blood when I wake up."

"I'm no catch."

"You're fantastic. You keep fighting. You sing. You know how to bloody *live*."

"Let's do that together then. Do our surviving *together*. I love you, Blue Murray. Could you love me, do you think?"

Blue kissed his palm. His wrist. His forehead. His closed eyes.

"I already do."

He held her with two strong arms. They kissed. He smiled against her lips.

"I think together we'll be bombproof."

34. Red-handed

Revelation that night was as simple as a swim in the River Lee and carrying K-Jam to shore.

John's shoulder ached afterwards. Even after a hot shower, in warm, dry clothes, he was stiff-jointed; clumsy.

His sketchbooks were in the pocket of his dressing gown. In fetching one, both tumbled out. He lurched for the incriminating one. It skittered beyond his awkward fingers…against Sherlock's slippered feet.

Sherlock, naturally, picked it up. But it had fallen open, face down, so as Sherlock lifted it, he saw.

Everything.

Intrigued, he turned page after page of John's secret drawings.

Sherlock's elegant hands, wise eyes. The graceful length of his legs. The sway and swell of his back and backside as he bent over his microscope.

John's adoration, admiration and desire were in every line.

John's heart was in his dry mouth.

"Sherlock…"

"I said I don't like to be touched; that relationships were detrimental to my work. You remember?"

"Vividly. I'm sor—"

"I've reassessed the data." Sherlock serenely handed the sketchbook to John. "I've an errand to run. While I'm gone, you should think about kissing me."

"…Oh?"

"I'll be thinking about kissing *you*."

Sherlock returned twenty minutes later.

"I've been thinking," said John huskily, eyes bright with hope. "Have you?"

"I have."

"May I kiss you?"

"Please."

And then Sherlock Holmes *blushed*.

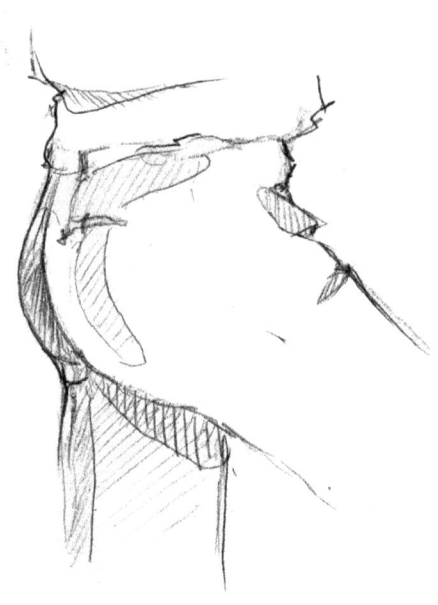

35. Shy

Sherlock Holmes wasn't shy. He was not that kind of man.

I once said that love was anathema to me, too. Yet here I am.

And here he was. *Shy.*

The colour was high on his sharp cheekbones. His fingers plucked nervously at each other. His lowered gaze and the teeth biting his lip were not coquettish or flirtatious. They spoke only of his sudden, shocking diffidence at the brash notion that he wanted to kiss John and had said so.

As Sherlock's fingers twisted, John's strong hand covered them and his thumb rubbed against Sherlock's knuckles.

If he says one patronising word, swore Sherlock, angry with his own self-conscious inhibitions. He had no idea how to complete the threat.

John was calm and centred, as always. He spoke not with patronising assurances but with soft and aching hope.

"You have the loveliest hands I've ever seen," said John.

Sherlock finally looked up.

"I've wanted to kiss you for weeks," John said.

Sherlock pressed his mouth to John's, and sighed into the perfection of the warm lips meeting his. He melted into the longed-for sensation of tongue-tips touching, the taste of shared breath.

They parted, reluctantly, holding hands, John's smile bright as fire. "You have the loveliest eyes, too."

"You're mistaken," murmured Sherlock, for surely John's brown eyes epitomised masculine beauty.

36. Not Shy

"Mistaken?" The creases of worry between John's eyebrows were as charming as his puzzled frowns always were.

Sherlock knew he was appalling at love talk; always had been. But he had mastered languages, deductive reasoning, chemistry, martial arts, and disguise. Last time, love had been unreciprocated, but he'd somehow stimulated more than simple fondness in this fine man's feelings. Surely, he could learn how to make love with deliberate words as well as unconscious deeds.

"*Your* eyes...are lovelier. They're kind. And they see something in me worth the value of your regard."

Fabulous. Now he was talking like an Edwardian parson.

But John seemed to like it, his worry blooming into a glowing smile. "Well, when you put it like that..."

"You should believe me," said Sherlock, grey eyes now sparkling, "I'm a stupendously clever man."

"You are."

"And I recognised all of your finest qualities almost immediately."

"Almost?"

"I was distracted briefly by my sheer good luck in finding such a perfect flatmate."

"Kiss me again."

Sherlock prided himself on knowing when to speak and when to hold his peace. Now he pressed his lips to John's again.

He marvelled at the pleasure of holding John in his arms; at being held. He deepened the kiss and their willing, warm bodies drew closer together. Heart thundering, Sherlock felt suddenly bold.

37. Bold

John's hands were against Sherlock's back, Sherlock's on John's hips, as they kissed.

What steps come next? Mutual nakedness, fathoming how to orchestrate their burgeoning erections, was a definite long-term goal, but it seemed precipitate in the midst of their first kiss.

Sherlock had moved too fast before, with crushing results.

Yet one of Sherlock's gifts was to conquer fear. So Sherlock, being Sherlock, boldly asked. "More?"

John, being John, prompted for illumination. "More of what?"

"More of you."

John's understanding may have been flawed, but he too was bold. He placed Sherlock's hands at the open top button of his shirt. "All right."

Sherlock unbuttoned John's shirt to reveal his throat, his chest. His fingers traced dips and ridges; beneath the shirt he found the bullet scar: a small dent in the flesh.

Sherlock's fingers trailed through the hair on John's chest (John's nipples tightened pleasingly) to his sternum. Back to the scar, a tender caress.

He might have died. I might never have known him. I might have been lonely forever.

A sudden sorrow must have filled his eyes. John took Sherlock's fingers; kissed them, pressed them with intuitive understanding against his carotid artery. Pulse elevated now, strong.

"Don't be sad. I'm here now. With you."

Sherlock brushed his thumb across that blessed pulse, and felt no longer bereft.

38. Seen

I was drunk on the taste of Sherlock's mouth; on his gasping breath. His body under my hands was strong, lithe, pliant: just as I'd always dreamed.

His gaze pierced me as always, that avid look he gave to the things that truly intrigued him. Being the subject of that scrutiny was heady. My scar bothered him, but soon his mouth was on me again—better than I'd imagined.

Then once more, he ran his gaze, his hands, over my chest. His beautiful hands cupped my shoulders then ran down my arms to my wrists, hands, palms and fingers. He studied those too.

I shivered. He hesitated.

"Keep going."

"It doesn't bother you. My…looking."

"You…ah…can probably tell how much I like it."

We both glanced down at my nascent erection. I loved that it made him grin with delight. With some trepidation too.

"I like you looking. I like that you *see* me," I told him. "Nobody's ever really seen me before."

Sherlock, frowning, brushed his fingers over my scar again.

"That doesn't count," I said. "He was killing the uniform. John Watson didn't matter to him at all. I'm mostly invisible to the clients too. I don't mind. Because *you* see me. And I feel…worth seeing."

He kissed my palm, my throat, my mouth. "You are, John. You are beguiling."

39. Knock Knock Knock

Sherlock yearned to explore his beguiling John.

He also yearned to withdraw into solitude. He was dizzy with the influx of data; with John's willingness to offer it to him.

"Are you all right?"

"Sorry. Yes. I just. I need. Time."

"Take whatever time you need."

John held Sherlock's hands; kissed them. (*Just as Blue had kissed K-Jam's. What did that mean about Blue and K-Jam? What did that mean about him and John?*)

Sherlock gently rebuttoned John's shirt (John let him). The gesture was surprisingly sensual.

A chaste kiss goodnight and they parted.

Lying, dressed, in bed, Sherlock listened to John move in his upstairs room. John's tread was different. Lighter. Rapidly tapping now. John—dancing?

Sherlock pressed a hand over the dancing tippety-tippety-tippety of his heart.

He'd left Mycroft last week having decided to seek evidence of reciprocation. Maybe in the sketchbook John so closely guarded.

And yes! It spilled over with evidence of John's passionate regard.

No wonder Sherlock had fled, overwhelmed, to pace Baker Street.

More dance-tapping from above. John's happiness, uncontained. Sherlock smiled ceiling-ward.

The tapping stopped. Then started: distinctive, deliberate—
repeated.

-.- .. ..

Sherlock seized a shoe and stood on his mattress. He
returned the Morse code message through his ceiling.

K I S S

Sherlock, grinning, dropped to the bed and bounced.

40. Oh What a Beautiful Morning

He's *shy*. Not usually, but last night, yes. Why is that so endearing? A grown man *blushing*.

Shy or not, he half stripped me, ran his hands over me, exploring. (He likes exploring; he's endlessly curious. That's endearing, too.)

My scar made him *sad*.

Then he seemed overcome. Not just shy. Inexperienced? Wary, certainly.

I want to make him feel safe.

I adore him.

I love him.

I'm not telling him *that*. If a kiss—he's a terrific kisser, really pays attention—overwhelms him, what would *that* admission do? Especially if he's not. You know. *In love* back.

Breathe, Watson. He wants this too, and there's time.

I went to my room and I *missed* him. Couldn't help a victory dance. *Please*, he'd said, and we kissed.

Went to bed alone, but we sent Morse code kisses to each other through my floor.

I had a lovely wank, thinking of him. His body is strong, lean; more responsive to touch than I'd dreamt. Oh god. I want him to touch me again. I want to kiss every part of him.

This morning he emerged practically waltzing. He kissed me while I made tea then danced off again, smile as big as the world. He dazzled me with a grin and said, "Let's track down this league of redheads together."

I'm *besotted*.

41. The Red-Headed League

"You said he'd drowned."

"I knocked him out. He's got no fucking legs. We threw him in the Lee and watched him sink. How could I know he'd swim out?"

"By *thinking*, Sebastian, you cretin."

"I'll go shoot him now if you like."

"Were you dropped on your head as a child? It's too fecking late now."

"Well fuck you, smartarse."

"That's *Professor* Smartarse, you little tick."

"Half the blame's Liam's. You won't call him names, though, will you? It'd be like calling *yourself* a moron."

"Speaking of whom, where is he?"

"Catching up with his black market contacts. You know him. Colonel Liam O'Rourke: *international entrepreneur.*"

"Does he have the goods?"

"I've got them. They were right under the floorboards, as promised. Prescott'll be furious when he gets out and finds we wormed into his old digs to pinch his stash."

"Then he should have kept his mouth shut when you shared his cell."

"Maybe we can pay him off. With a cut of the auction proceeds. Oh, fuck yer pissy face. I'm *joking.*"

"Very funny. It might be easier to discreetly dispatch him before his release."

"Seb! James! Gis a kiss, ya smelly eejits."

"Liam! Feck off, you dopey spanner."

"Liam. You're late."

"How's about ye, Professor? Get that stick out yer arse. And stop needling our baby bro."

42. Omniscient

"Have the activities of two redheads from Belfast crossed your path?" Sherlock asked before I'd even removed my coat. "Named Seb and Liam." His cheeks were ruddy with excited activity.

"Let's talk in the parlour."

"Confining the disruption to the Stranger's Room?" he riposted cheekily, recalling the only room in which I'd speak to others during my diffident childhood.

Sherlock: cheeky? He was full of robust energy and preening confidence. No trace of last week's melancholy remained.

Slight stubble rash below his lip; the imperfect fall of hastily combed hair; shirt awry. He'd been thoroughly kissed in the last few hours. His eyes danced as he saw that I'd seen.

"I call it the Diogenes Club now, for I'm called on day or night for cynical advice on a mistrustful world."

Sherlock touched my wrist, kindly.

"Sebastian Moran might be your man," I said. "A disgraced army major with known criminal associates."

Over tea, Sherlock told me of his case; I shared what intelligence I could. He left with the bit between his teeth. "John and I have much to do!"

I detected lingering uncertainty. His own demons, no doubt.

I've no need to deliver a 'hurt my brother at your peril' speech. But after Musgrave, I swear, if Watson hurts my brother, none will find where I've buried his body.

43. Kiss and Tell

John Watson	Violet "Blue" Murray
Ever heard of a Major Sebastian Moran?	
	Is this one of the bastards that attacked Kris?
Could be. Our source says he has known criminal associates.	
	R U serious?
The source is Sherlock's highly connected brother, so yeah. Serious. Moran's ex-army. Military engineer. Blows shit up.	
	Fuck me.
Ta, but I've got a boyfriend now.	
	Trixie, you sly dog!
;)	Your detective finally saw the light, huh?
Saw my sketches of him anyway. Dead giveaway I fancy him.	
	Good on you. While we're confessing, K-Jam and I are finally official.
About time!	:-P We figure we can be crazy in tandem.
Works best for all of us, I think.	
	I'll let him know about this

Moran fucker.

Careful though. The other one, Liam, might also be ex-army. Another redhead. Different surname, but Sherlock thinks they might be related.

That's a lot of names.

Tip of the iceberg, Sherlock says. Seb Moran's the only one we've got a picture of—he did time for possession of a concealed knife. On purpose, Sherlock says, to find out what his forger cellmate had hidden in K-Jam's flat.

You've worked fast in two days!

What can I say? My bloke is a genius.

Yeah, but mine can sing.

Give him a kiss from me, then.

You kiss your own bloke.

44. Lost

I still crackled with rage that Kris had suffered so criminals could retrieve counterfeiting plates. Million dollar American treasury bonds, Sherlock rationalised, were *worth* that murderous effort.

That's unfair. He wasn't excusing it, only explaining motives, seeking a trail. The knowledge led us to an accomplice in Woodcote. Pia d'Angelo, not-so-reformed crafter of forgery-quality paper stock.

No-one answered our knock. Sherlock opened the unlocked door. We saw a woman lying in a blood-soaked kitchen.

Triage was useless. She was hours dead, wrist torn by the broken glass in her hand. I retreated to the hall. Sherlock explored with his loupe; called Lestrade.

Eventually: "John?"

I touched a photograph of the late Pia and a girl. "She looks like Alice."

I'd told Sherlock about Mary and Alice. Did he recall how I'd stumbled over saying 'my daughter'?

"This child's safe at school," Sherlock said gently. So like him. Clinical sometimes, but at heart kind.

Lestrade arrived.

"Looks like suicide," Sherlock advised. "It isn't. It's linked to the Jambur case."

Sherlock's deductions flew: red hairs on her clothes, glass shards in the sink. She'd fought.

He kept glancing at me. I nodded. *I'm fine.*

I'd survived a war to find Mary had moved on. No forwarding address. For the first time since I'd held and kissed that baby girl, I'd miss her birthday.

45. Like a Bee to the Bloom

John was pensive the remainder of the day after Pia d'Angelo's murder, moodily sketching then abandoning portraits of the absent Alice.

Sherlock distracted him with the pursuit of criminals.

The evening's ill-advised and probably illegal entry into a deserted lock-up that was nothing of the sort (rusted door; new padlock) produced the best result: the seizing of forged bonds paper stock.

A laggard sentry attacked them with a crowbar. John disarmed him with protective speed. His triumph stirred Sherlock's passions. Rather than letting desire distract him, Sherlock let it fire him up. *Rewards come after successes.*

Leaving Lestrade and her team to tidy up the loose ends, Sherlock and John took the DLR and Circle Line home to snatch a few hours' sleep. The next day they followed elusive threads, learned names, heard rumours, but found nothing concrete. The trail had gone suddenly cold.

Despite John's apparent support, Sherlock's failure weighed on him.

He'll grow bored. I must do better. I must <u>scintillate.</u>

That evening, Sherlock would have offered unbridled affection, only sudden shyness robbed him of momentum.

Sherlock's diffidence revived John from his introspection. He pulled Sherlock onto his lap; kissed him. Cuddled, face snugged into Sherlock's throat, wanting only the comforting companionship of touch.

Sherlock melted into John's embrace; contentment slow-humming in his veins like a summer honeybee buzz.

46. Anticipation

25 March
To buy:
- *Chapstick*
- *Condoms*
- *Lubricant*

Precipitous? Not yet. Soon. Be prepared!

A week to be certain. (Stupid to be cautious? Wise?)

J has recovered from yesterday's melancholy. More demonstrative yet doesn't push.

His patience is erotic.

D'Angelo's murder; 14 hours yesterday in pubs, off-licences, bookies, fishing for rumours.

Results:

  −   suggestions of one coordinating mind
  −   sitting close on the Tube, nipples stiff at heat of J's thigh against mine.

Why am I waiting?

James. Liam. Sebastian. Moran. O'Rourke. Moriarty. Colonel. Major. 6 names, 2 titles.

Nothing adds up.

On the Tube, J spoke quietly to me. I leaned close to hear.

"We'll ask Blue about this Colonel and the Major."

My cock went stiff as my nipples. J could recite football scores to the same effect. His voice. His scent. His breath on my skin. Thigh against my thigh. Less what he said than unsaid promises underneath.

Why am I waiting FFS? ~~He might change his mind~~

At home, made my notes; J openly drew my profile. How is *this* erotic?

Invited him onto the lounge. I dithered. *Shy.*

J held me on his lap. We kissed. My hands in his hair. His face warm against my throat. No demands. Not sexual; yet erotic.

~~I am still hard.~~

Can I manage 11 more days with a permanent boner?

47. Squad Goals

K-Jam was singing when John arrived at the pub with Sherlock. Blue saluted them with a beer while cheering K-Jam's passionate karaoke finale of 'Defying Gravity'.

"My round!" declared Blue when K-Jam wheeled off the stage.

Sherlock observed the group. Egg had a prosthetic arm. Jeeves seemed as unscathed as Blue, but his body language indicated his unseen wounds were as deep.

Jeeves shook Sherlock's hand warmly. "You saved our K-Jam. You'll do right by our Trixie, yeah?"

"Jambur saved himself," asserted Sherlock, "John…"

"Is fine," interrupted John. "We're still looking into K-Jam's case."

Sherlock explained what he knew of Major Sebastian Moran, which was almost nothing.

"John suggests you may help us gather intelligence through the army grapevine." Sherlock sensed hesitation. "There's a nominal stipend in it for you, of course."

Egg scowled at him. "Charity, is it noo?"

Sherlock didn't flinch. "You have knowledge and networks I lack. Recompensing people for their expertise isn't charity."

"Aye, and what are we to do?" Egg asked.

"Ask questions. Visit army clubs. Listen for buzz about Sebastian Moran or this Liam."

"Standard KISS operation," grinned Jeeves.

"Keep It Simple, Stupid," Blue and K-Jam chorused.

"A'right. I'll be one o' yer Greenfly Irregulars," the Scot agreed gruffly, citing the nickname for army intelligence, "And when we find him, we'll wallop the scabby bawbag."

48. Treasure

While 'walloping the scabby bawbag' was a good goal, John convinced his mates that reporting intel was wiser. Jeeves proudly declared them the Baker Street Irregulars, and they drank to that.

Hours later, they returned home. Sherlock checked the veterans' chatrooms where John had left subtle queries. No response.

On the sofa, they snogged, handsy. When Sherlock stopped on the brink of sex, John relaxed into a contented cuddle. He nosed Sherlock's dark hair. "How'd you start all this detecting, then?"

"School," Sherlock said. "I identified the neighbour who'd sent threatening letters to my friend Victor's father."

"Clever." John kissed his temple.

More warily, Sherlock said, "Then the Musgrave Treasure at University."

John, tipsy, sensed Sherlock's anxiety without understanding it. He squeezed Sherlock, not tight but comforting. "S'okay."

"One summer, I tutored Reginald Musgrave in chemistry at Musgrave Hall. I solved an old family riddle: a wordy treasure map. Found a box of papers, of mere historical value."

Sherlock didn't tell John about afternoons naked in the hayloft with Reggie; or of Reggie's scorn after he found the 'treasure'.

"Love, Holmes? Unless you're doing your party trick you're a bore. I've no use for smartarse *staff*. Fuck off. You're an embarrassment."

Sherlock didn't say what happened after.

But he closed his eyes while John held him, and didn't feel so broken.

49. Precipitous

For three days, Sherlock was *scintillating*. A run of puzzles, small and large, brought by random clients and DI Lestrade, were dispatched with *élan*. Sherlock's natural grace erupted in flourishing gestures, gentlemanly bows, dancing feet.

John stood with him, ever-present back-up, lending physical and moral authority to their dealings. Whenever their eyes met, they sparkled; wordless communication of delight in each other.

(Lestrade consulted Sherlock less from necessity than the fond curiosity of witnessing two men falling in love.)

Only the matter of the redheads eluded Sherlock. Homicidal Moran and his dangerous mate Liam had gone to ground. Frustrating.

Buoyed by the discovery of the 'stolen' jewels secreted in a plaster bust (insurance fraud, terribly dull), John and Sherlock walked across Regent's Park, holding hands.

At their front door, Sherlock was reluctant to let go. John, with a grin, kissed Sherlock's fingers, clasped in his, and managed the keys left-handed.

In their living room, Sherlock still held to John's hand then, feeling foolish, let go, blushing. Shy again.

Determined to not be shy, Sherlock pulled John close, kissed him. John, arms around Sherlock, approved with a throaty hum.

Sherlock kissed him soft-slow; lip-nibbled along his jaw; suckled his earlobe. John sigh-moaned, offered up his throat for tasting.

Then Sherlock froze, breathing hard.

"We're a week ahead of schedule," he lamented. "*Bugger.*"

50. L'amour est un oiseau rebelle

"Schedule?" John was curious; wary.

Do better. "Two weeks after the first kiss seemed more decorous."

Sherlock was *blushing* again.

John smiled, tenderly fond. "There's no rush."

"Our mutual erections suggest otherwise."

"I'm game to update the schedule if you are." John caressed Sherlock's cheek. "Or we can wait."

Sherlock nudged into the touch. "Seven days is decorous enough."

John leaned in; kissed Sherlock soft and deep. A kiss full of care, devotion, passion.

Like the kiss in my dream.

Sherlock's body arched voluptuously towards John. Dream-memory and present sensation interwove, leaving Sherlock feeling peculiarly out-of-body yet grounded.

John melted against him. He tugged Sherlock's shirt free, made him shiver with fingertip trails on his spine.

"Please," John murmured; suckled on Sherlock's earlobe.

"Yes," replied Sherlock, without knowing what John wanted, or what *he* did. Only more of this. *Please.* This closeness, this touch. He was hungry for it. Starving.

In Sherlock's bedroom they stripped each other naked. Thirsty gazes were slaked with explorations, using hands, mouths, tongues, on luscious curves, pale planes, old scars, new, and yearning upthrust hardness. A soft-chanted litany of *please* and *yes* led to soft-grunting pleasure, gasping cries, little subsiding sighs of bliss.

John cuddled into Sherlock after. Sherlock, satisfied as a cat, drew patterns on John's skin, contentedly humming Bizet's *Habanera*.

Love's a rebellious bird.

51. Right Now

I awoke, exquisitely lethargic, Sherlock's bare body pressed against mine. We smelled of sweat, sex, serenity. I kissed the crown of his head. He mumbled a good morning.

I think he was feeling coy again: funny and endearing, considering we'd been licking each other's balls.

He's been stop-and-go all week, but so have I. I died in Afghanistan, briefly. Blue saved me, but it took meeting Sherlock to properly begin living again. I'm hungry for life now, for him, but not *greedy* for it. *Now* isn't as good as *right*. Last night was finally *right*.

"Shower," I said, taking his hand. Sherlock turned from coy to brazen on a pin, as he does. (God, I love that.)

My hair curls in steam. Sherlock commented on it as he soaped me up under the water, his touch as captivated as his tone.

I'm not the man I was, physically, though I'm much restored. Sherlock's beautiful, though. Long-limbed, lean, graceful. I washed him too, sudsy hands slipping over his thighs, chest, the scars on his arms (I could weep for those). His rising cock. He clutched my arse (God I love that). Kissed me like he needed it. Like I need him. (God, *oh God*, I love him.)

He pressed me to the tiles; we wanked each other to orgasm. And now—breakfast!

52. The Sapper

Seb balanced on the ladder, elbow hooked around a rung, ignoring the stinking water trickling below him through the tunnels.

Rats chittered.

"Shut yer bake, ya feckers," he said as he tamped explosives into cracks into the brickwork underneath d'Angelo's second paper hidey-hole.

Seb'd enjoyed blowing shite up in the army, till he got fed up with hierarchy. Liam, Colonel by then, scooped him out of trouble, then got him back in it in Belfast. They'd two heists under their belts when Professor James Moriarty called.

Unlike Liam, Seb hadn't been thrilled by their missing brother's return.

Seb was sorry Mam had to give up her first bubs, being only 15; and feck the gobshites who buggered the paperwork. No wonder Mam couldn't find James after she married Da. She got Liam back; James was lost.

But James'd done all right.

The rats scattered as Seb retreated down the tunnel a-ways.

Detonation.

Crunch. Crack. Puff of dust, hiss of water from broken pipes.

Seb grinned. Over the week, leaking water and fractured foundations would flood and ruin d'Angelo's stash. Artificial scarcity, James called it.

"James Moriarty can kiss my arse."

Seb sauntered to Target Two. He didn't calculate the future like his brothers, but he was a brilliant army engineer. He could make things go exactly the right kind of *boom*.

53. Scandal

My darling Norton,

Lizzie will deliver this letter by hand. My office, house, car and dressing room were all searched. I can't be sure Will's people didn't bug everything.

As we predicted, Will engaged that well-regarded PI, Sherlock Holmes.

After my final performance of *Dr Jekyll; Ms Hyde*, the stage door crowd was huge. Big clue there. I'm not *that* popular! When they suddenly jostled me, a blond man and a self-proclaimed autograph-hound steadied me as someone shouted about an engagement ring on the ground.

I pressed a hand to my shirt to be sure it was still under there on its chain, before realising it was a trick. My 'fan' was certainly Holmes of Baker Street.

To prove it, I went ahead to Baker Street in a fake beard. ;-) Guess who was there? My 'fan' and the blond, kissing on the doorstep. So smug, celebrating their 'victory' for William Ormstein, the bastard Prince of Grünewald, who broke off our engagement as soon as he got a richer offer. If he hadn't inscribed the ring with both our names, we wouldn't be in this mess. Or, considering he's insanely possessive despite dumping me, maybe we would.

I can't believe I ever thought I loved him.

Thank God for you!

Till tonight,

Yours, heart and soul,

Irene (Your loving bride!)

54. Offence

Sherlock deduced Ormstein was no saint when Ormstein arrived in disguise and paid five grand up-front for expenses. He'd taken the case for curiosity, but the magnitude of his error was soon clear.

Will Ormstein broke my heart, then imprisoned me in Grünewald, insisting I remain as his mistress, read Adler's letter.

I escaped, but he's pursued me relentlessly. He claims I'm trying to stop his royal wedding. As if I'd want him. Now I love and am loved by a far better man. We're leaving England for a new life. I keep that ring to keep us safe.

Irene Godfrey, nee Adler.

Confronted at Baker Street, Grünewald's monarch denied and then excused his actions. Fruitless threats followed; he left in no doubt of their contempt.

Sherlock was ashamed. This case failed the Ritual. *Did I help someone? Hurt anyone?* No. Yes. Worse, he'd dragged the Irregulars into that farce at the theatre.

Sherlock expected John's scorn, but John saved that for Ormstein.

"Plausible prick. Can we do anything about him?"

"Oh, yes. One kind of iniquity usually indicates another."

A month of meticulous investigation later, Ormstein's rich fiancée denounced him. His arrest for corruption and bribery followed. His sister, Thilde, took the throne.

John's celebratory kiss didn't abate Sherlock's unease.

Do better. If he leaves, you've only yourself to blame.

55. Trixie

After the Adler case, Sherlock manfully apologised to the Irregulars at their Debriefing-and-Karaoke night at The Stormy Petrel.

"Ne'er mind," said Egg. "Last command fuck-up cost me an arm. This one paid a pony! Your shout."

Next round, they shared the scuttlebutt.

"Major Moran got sprung black marketeering," reported K-Jam, "Turns out Colonel O'Rourke's his half-brother. O'Rourke pulled strings to ship Moran home before charges were laid."

"My mate Ron Adair at the Moth Club says Moran's been barred for card-sharping," added Jeeves.

Next round was on Egg. "Fur challenge, Trix!" he declared. The squad promptly chugged their beers while John sketched furiously. Glasses slammed down, he stopped. He'd drawn a walrus.

"That's Egg!"

Next, John drew a cockatoo.

"Captain Bulstrode!"

Then a greyhound.

"Easy-peasy! That's Cluedo, here."

"Kiss for the winner," hooted K-Jam, kissing Blue.

"Cluedo?" Sherlock asked.

"You've earned it," grinned Blue.

"I see," Sherlock's eyes shone, on the trail. "Tell me: K-Jam's gun famously jammed?"

"Four times in training."

"Jeeves. Named for the literary valet. Your surname's Butler."

Jeeves doffed an invisible cap.

"Egg Burns," continued Sherlock. "Scotch Egg."

"These Sassenachs think it's hilarious."

"Blue, as in 'violets are…'."

"Nope. Sarge gave me a mock Oxford Rowing Blue for sinking a canoe."

Undeterred, Sherlock tapped John's art. "You're named for that artist, Potter. Trixie is short for Beatrix."

56 Thinking Aid

8 April
- *Clean tea-stains from carpet*
- *Replace broken teacup*

NB:
- *Hungover J has nightmares*
- *5am violin doesn't help*
- *J apologised 3 times for throwing cup*
- *Make-up sex is as good as people claim*
- *My post-sex thinking less disciplined; poss. more stimulated?*

Moran assaulted K-Jam to steal plates. Murdered d'Angelo? Forged paper/ink barrels destroyed in 2 locations.
- Volume/state of wreckage conveniently disguises original stock amnts
  - Anything missing?
  - Why remove stock?
- Authorities aware of the plates.
  - Regardless, plates not useless
  - Brothers could still print fake bonds; sell materials to 3rd party
  - US bonds. American buyers? Middle Eastern & Sth American also likely.
- Mycroft's Moran dossier suggests he lacks foresight for a plan like this. Liam O'Rourke's army record suggests he's smarter. Counter argument: his involvement in Kris' assault.
- Who is the Moriarty whispered of from Tower Hamlets to Chelsea?
  - O'Rourke & Moran are half-brothers. Investigate further family links.

8/4 noon

J brought tea. Apologised again re cup. Doesn't count nightmare as mitigating.

I apologised for violin. Thinking music, I said. Reported positive effect of sex on my thinking.

"In future I'll skip the violin & go straight to shagging," I promised.

Made him laugh: led to kissing; further excellent sex.

Updating journal as J sleeps beside me. He's glorious: sheet askew, sunlight on his lovely bare bottom.

57. Red Herring

The mid-morning students crossed Exhibition Road, burdened with backpacks and parental expectations, dashing through the campus for lectures, tutorials, or the library beyond Queen's Lawn.

Sherlock affected their loping walk, fledgling energy and youthful distraction. He'd dressed in dark jeans, ironic 90s T-shirt, duffle coat. John had ruffled his straight, dark hair so that it flopped over one eye, declared him a master of disguise, and kissed him goodbye as he set off on his mission.

Sherlock recalled the greenness of his own university years studying chemistry (and the painful reason he hadn't graduated) and brought it all to his convincing persona.

Relaxed post-coital stream-of-consciousness had led Sherlock to this campus, following the Moriarty whisper-trail.

Sherlock had sought frayed threads from the tangle of this counterfeiting case. Consulting with Lestrade, he examined loose ends from other cases, solved and unsolved, tinged with Seb Moran's *modus operandi*.

A superb mind, the whispers said. Disciplined and calculating. Ruthless and relentless.

This unremarkable Chair in Applied Mathematics at the Imperial College London was only one of several potential criminal masterminds on his list.

As he sat at the back of the Pippard lecture theatre, Sherlock ruefully decided this bland specimen wasn't his quarry, while mild-mannered Professor Moriarty tugged at his beard and spoke at monotonous length on the economics of auctions and combinatorial bidding.

58. Temper, Temper

Sounds of splintering crockery in 221A were audible from 221B.

"It transpires Ms Hudson and her girlfriend have the same boyfriend," explained Sherlock.

"Hell." John laughed.

"You don't have a secret girlfriend, do you?" Sherlock teased.

Laughter died. "Why would you say that?"

Sherlock's skin prickled. "You were married."

John bristled. "Mary and I'd dated at school. I wasn't ready to come out, and she was my best friend. When she got pregnant, her Catholic parents threw her out. So we got married."

"I see."

"I was determined not to be gay back then. I was stupid, Sherlock, but never straight and not bisexual."

"John…"

"I don't have or want a secret girlfriend." John snatched up his coat; hunched into it. "Back in a bit." He slammed the door behind him.

John's usually very even-tempered, Sherlock considered. *Teacup episode notwithstanding. Subjects touching on his past rattle him, though. Hugh; his wife and daughter.*

Holmes, you're an insensitive ass.

But then: *he walked away from a ruined marriage; from an irredeemable brother. Will he ever walk away from me?*

Less than an hour later, John returned, contrite and bearing gifts: a new teacup and Sherlock's favoured rosin.

Kisses asking for and bestowing forgiveness became passionate. Sighs became earthy laughter as John unzipped Sherlock's trousers with the promise to 'rosin up his bow'.

59. Army Rat

John splashed through the noisome water at Sherlock's heels, breathing shallowly through his mouth.

Sherlock surmised Moran had removed some of d'Angelo's counterfeit stocks before destroying the remainder. Seeking evidence, they were investigating the sewer tunnels he'd used to flood the storehouses.

Sherlock complained that the Met and Thames Water's operations had obliterated clues, but he'd found traces, which he followed like a bloodhound.

Rats squealed; scurried into the darkness.

"Watch these bastards don't take your nose off," John joked as Sherlock bent close to the brickwork with his torch, "I'm fond of your nose. And the rest of you."

Sherlock, fully aware of John's lovingly rendered sketches of his hawk-like profile (remembering his warm mouth kissing Sherlock's whole body last night), straightened. "This way."

They continued by the combined torchlight, Sherlock periodically stopping to closely inspect scuffs in the brickwork.

An hour later, Sherlock shone his torch on signs of a recent ascent. They followed. Emerged by a footpath. A pedestrian skirted them and their insalubrious smell.

"Where are we?" John asked.

"Hackney Grove, parallel to Mare Street."

"Do you know *every* street in London?"

"Very nearly. One guess on Moran's last known address."

"Hackney?"

"Yes. Also home—"

"To the ex-servicemen's club that barred Moran."

"Exactly. Inconclusive, but indicative."

"What now?"

"We set a trap for the little beggar."

60. Simpatico

Sherlock and his *inamorato* visited today. After introductions, Doctor Watson stood patiently by while Sherlock and I conversed.

Oh, but he covertly inspected me as I did him!

His subtle curiosity was soon abandoned, his eye returning to Sherlock. Despite laudable attempts at parade-ground blankness, he gazed on Sherlock as though upon an endlessly rewarding *objet d'art*. More. Watson's demeanour speaks of deep tenderness as well as earthier appreciation.

Watson clearly adores Sherlock. I'd commend him for that alone, but he also presents as a man of strong character, courage, and constancy.

I undertook to investigate this Colonel O'Rourke. "Your Irregulars are proving useful."

"Good people," agreed Sherlock. Watson glowed with dignified pride at the praise for his friends. Sherlock, observing, was indulgently amused. Watson laughed self-deprecatingly. Sherlock smiled in turn. Such simpatico!

Sherlock once bitterly declared that love (and lust) were mere distractions, sapping intellectual rigour. His recent casework and air of louche tranquillity belie the argument.

"Love agrees with you," I murmured as they departed.

"It enhances my understanding of motives," he admitted cagily.

"Bunkum. You're positively *nipped* with intellectual rigour." Referring imprudently to a just-visible love-bite.

Sherlock blushed to his hairline. As, alas, did I.

Fortunately, Watson steadfastly declined to notice.

"Pleasure to meet you, Mycroft," he said, with obvious sincerity.

I increasingly approve of my brother's beau.

61. Rat Trap

I slept in my own bed for the first time in three weeks. I didn't want Sherlock feeling constrained as he paced and muttered all night (it helps him think). He's been understanding about the Teacup Incident, but still.

"You slept poorly," he observed come morning.

"Shoulder's playing up." I didn't want to admit I'd felt lonely without him.

Mycroft, surely more than a senior civil servant, had provided curious intel on Colonel Liam O'Rourke. O'Rourke had left the army six months after Moran and subsequently disappeared from Belfast.

Bizarrely, no paper or electronic images of him remained on file. A week after the security breach deleting them all, administrative Corporal Melanie Porlock was hit by a freight train in Retford.

Yet another murder.

"Any progress?"

"Perhaps," said Sherlock. He's bloody cagey sometimes. He loves his *ta-da* moments: goddamned sexy with them, too.

"You have secret plans, do you?" I pressed close, thigh between his legs, arms round his waist.

"Yes." His lips teased mine, but no kiss for me. "But rewards come after successes."

Two can play that glorious game. I firmly fondled his crotch. (I can be properly motivational.)

He grabbed my hand, kissed the palm, whirled away.

"Former Corporal Adair and I are setting a trap for Moran," he declared.

"Jeeves' mate Ron?"

"Now an Irregular."

"How?"

"Blackmail."

62. Set Up

Lestrade lurked beside Sherlock in Embankment Gardens, watching nearby York Watergate, the Thames' former shoreline.

"I'm not happy," muttered Lestrade.

"Adair volunteered. Moran cheated him of £2000." Sherlock peered Thames-wards. "And John's with him."

"*Also* a civilian."

Movement was visible on the peaked roof of a toilet block close to Victoria Embankment.

The DI spoke into her two-way. "Positions."

The Irregulars had spread rumours that Adair knew details of Moran's *underground hobbies*. Four grand for his silence. This morning's text stated: *10pm. York Watergate.*

Sherlock watched Adair and John navigate the crowded Watergate Walk towards the rendezvous.

Watergate Way's too crowded for a close-range assault. Shooting Adair from further away makes more sense. But Moran's roof's too steep, close and visible. Oh, hell…

"John! Get him out of there!"

Too late. Adair, jostled by a stranger in a hoodie, cried out.

Sherlock and Lestrade raced to John's location.

"Superficial cut over the hip," John reported, his hands and Adair's undershirt bloody, "Thank God for the armoured vest, Sherlock." A contingency plan, worn under Adair's windbreaker, it had deflected the blade.

"Wasn't Moran," grunted Adair, "Taller; had a moustache."

"Roof's clear," growled Lestrade. "We were *played.*"

Sherlock snarled his frustration.

"Except for the knife," grinned John, nodding at the object tangled in the bloodstained coat.

Sherlock could've kissed him. "A Filipino balisong!"

63. Failure

"You used *my knife* on the gabby prick?"

"They already know about you." Liam shrugged, "James decided it restricted the evidence pool if it were banjaxed."

"Which it fecking *were*. Or was that the idea? Is this a fit-up, Liam?"

"You think I'd do that?" Liam was genuinely outraged. "I threw my army career to the dogs for you, *big lad*."

Seb was instantly contrite. "God, Liam, I know. I'm sorry."

Liam squeezed Seb's shoulder. "I know you think he doesn't like you. But we weren't expecting Adair to have body armour. It's a setback, but not a failure. James'll think of something."

"He's not bloody *god*."

"You're an eejit," said Liam fondly. He ruffled Seb's hair, making Seb scowl and squirm in equal measure. "Don't be jealous, Sebby. He grew up alone, but after Mam got me back, I had you. So stop making a face like a cat's hoop."

Seb grumbled on for form's sake. "And my knife?"

"Your prints aren't on it. Quit yer gurning." Another affectionate scruffing of Seb's hair followed, and a wet, smacking kiss to his forehead. "Lay low. I always look after you, don't I?"

Seb was peculiarly calmed by being treated like he was 12 years old again. James was new family, but he and Liam were always going to be sibling besties.

64. Encouraged

Sherlock gazed out the window onto nothing.

I failed. I'm a failure.

He ignored John speaking until John stood directly in front of him.

"Come on, you, it's not so bad," John persisted.

"I exposed Adair to unwarranted danger, to no end. It's inexcusable."

"Ron wanted in. He's hardly scratched, he grabbed the knife, and he nearly grabbed that slippery bugger too. Besides, you didn't see him after."

Sherlock raised an eyebrow.

"He was re-energised. Like me after I met you."

I'm missing something.

"Civilian life's all you think of out there," John continued, "But for some of us…this ordinary life feels alien, like we're not part of it any more. It can be hard. But now the Irregulars feel they're contributing something important again. Ron was sinking. Now he sees options. He's talked to Lestrade about joining the Met. You've given him a gift."

"Oh."

John's nose brushed along his jaw, kisses following.

John Watson is not Reggie Musgrave.

"No rewards before success," murmured Sherlock without conviction.

"No successes without encouragement," countered John. Their lips met, yearning; hungry.

Self-recriminations melted away. "John," Sherlock murmured against John's mouth, "Would you be afraid to sleep with an idiot; a man whose mind has lost its grip?"

"Nope," laughed John, arms wrapped around Sherlock.

"Thank goodness."

"You've got this, Sherlock. Tomorrow's another battle."

65. Breakthrough

I spent the afternoon with the Irregulars, seeking leads on Moran and O'Rourke through the network, hoping they'd come to fruition.

Sherlock welcomed me home with an ebullient kiss, and news.

"The knife's not Filipino. The watermarks prove it was made in Sheffield by one William Morton in 1873. Butterfly knife sales are restricted under the Offensive Weapons Act, unless it's an antique. Assuming it wasn't a family heirloom, I approached an antique weapons dealer of my acquaintance."

"The bloke who sold you that American Civil War jack-knife you use to murder the bills?" Which were pinned to the mantelpiece with the bone-handled Winchester.

"And my loupe."

His grin lit fires in me, as always. "What did he say?"

"His friend of a friend of a friend sold this particular knife two years ago to Sebastian O'Rourke of 51 Warwick Road, Earl's Court."

His eyes sparkled impishly. I knew I was missing something.

"He's not still there, surely?"

"Perhaps. If he ever was." At my continued incomprehension he added, "It's the address of the east exit of Earl's Court tube station, John."

"That weird rotunda?"

"Exactly. I've been researching the building's various refurbishments and current tenants. That exit contains a curious feature: an empty room labelled The Historical Research Centre."

Understanding dawned, and I grinned too. "Sounds like an excellent bolthole."

66. Dancing Men

Like the Irregulars, I'm thriving on being part of Sherlock's world.

(I awoke to Sherlock kissing my neck, back, shoulders. Even the scar. I'd thought my life was over; now it can't possibly get better.)

On with the case. The area around the 'Historical Research Centre' was *too* clean.

"Moran's here," Sherlock asserted. Before telling Lestrade, though, Sherlock intended to learn more.

Sherlock spent days walking the station concourses (altering his look with clothes, posture and gait: what an actor he'd have been). I monitored the bolthole.

Day three he revealed his discovery: lines of stick figures along the bottom of the Service Announcements whiteboard. Different lines, different penmanship. One person drew during the day; the other at night.

To keep Sherlock's profile low, the Irregulars took over surveilling the exchanges. My contribution was noting the groceries, including crisps and malt bread, left by the door. Sherlock was unimpressed at first.

Our flat was festooned with copies of the messages in chronological order. He'd filled in Es based on frequency.

I puzzled over the message predating the food delivery. "Looks like a list."

Sherlock's eyes lit up. Under ⫟𝑋𝑋𝑋 he wrote VEDA. *Irish malt bread.*

He cracked the code through 'Taytos', 'Bushmills', 'cheese', 'marmalade' and 'Polos'.

The final messages:
𝑋𝑋⫟𝑋𝑋𝑋𝑋 𝑋𝑋𝑋⫟𝑋𝑋𝑋𝑋𝑋 𝑋𝑋𝑋 𝑋𝑋𝑋𝑋
Patie𝑋ce. E𝑋tractio𝑋 pla𝑋 soo𝑋.
𝑋𝑋𝑋𝑋𝑋⫟ 𝑋𝑋
Better be.

67. Liam and James

"Your brother…."

"*Our* brother, James."

"*Our* brother, Liam, is excellent at explosives and shooting things, but I cannot fathom how he ever made Major."

"Seb does a good sideline in blackmail. That and selective arse-kissing are handy in getting recommendations for promotion."

"He's a liability."

"Fuck you, James. Is Seb right? Did you set him up by getting me to use that knife?"

"No, I kept you safe in the event everything went south."

"And it did, because Adair was protected. Seb should have shot him like he planned."

"Seb needs to stop being an impulsive moron. Don't worry. You love him, so I'll look out for him. I've got an exit arranged, but he won't take instruction from me. Leave him a message for Friday night. In the meantime, I'm making inquiries into this persistent pest."

"Lestrade?"

"Lord, no. She's a plod like all the others. This private detective, Holmes. His flatmate's an army veteran. More than a flatmate, it seems. I'm looking into how to make him desist before it's necessary to dispose of him too."

"Shooting's easier."

"But it isn't smart. D'Angelo, despite her name, was no angel. A trail of nobler bodies, however, and the law gets much testier. You handle Seb. I'll handle everything else."

"The fake bond auction?"

"Of course. I already have six bidders."

68. Busker

In the passage from Warwick Road to the Earl's Court concourse, Sherlock played violin. He layered the amplified performance via a loop pedal. He plucked parts of Pachelbel's *Canon*, added melody and harmony lines, his whole body swaying.

Coins jangled into his case.

He reset the looper, layered new songs: *Under Pressure;* the *Games of Thrones* theme; Prince's *Kiss*.

Throughout, John sat on the ground opposite, sketching Sherlock's graceful lines. Whenever Sherlock indicated a passer-by of interest with his moving bow, John obediently strove to capture their likeness in a few neat strokes, adding details if they loitered.

One subject was a tall, slender, redheaded man, with a moustache and the bearing of a hunter. Four times he'd stalked past so far.

The fifth time he passed, glaring at the station notice whiteboard he couldn't approach unseen, he saw John working.

"Are you bloody drawing me?" Belfast accent.

John had swiftly flipped the page. He feigned innocence. "Nope."

"You fucking *are* drawing me."

John displayed his sketch: the violinist. Impressionist, capturing motion, music. "Why would I draw you when I've got him?"

The man scowled and departed.

At home, Sherlock studied the stealth portraits of his likely suspects.

"Well, now!"

"What?"

Sherlock recalled the dull lecture he'd attended at Pippard lecture hall.

"This must be O'Rourke. Professor Moriarty's doppelganger, *sans* beard."

69. Step Up

Sherlock easily deciphered the dancing men signalling an 8am Friday escape.

Lestrade wasn't amused by Sherlock, but forgave him because of the quality intel. Evidence was strong against Moran and accumulating on O'Rourke. Professor Moriarty was the Joker in the pack, but he was on their radar now.

7am Friday, Lestrade's team watched all exits, aiming to capture both Moran and O'Rourke.

At 7:49 it went tits-up with the announcement of a bomb threat and a call to calmly evacuate the station. Commuters crowded from the exits, more exasperated than alarmed. Moran was certainly among them but remained concealed by the mob.

Worse, the Met confirmed that the unaccompanied parcel found on the Piccadilly eastbound platform was a nail bomb. Unprimed, but genuine.

"Moran assembled this before going to ground," concluded Sherlock sourly, furious with himself at another failure. "The architect of all this plans several branching pathways ahead. We must do better than catch up. Have you found Moran's mother yet, Lestrade?"

"Mrs Moran took a month-long cruise last week," Lestrade reported, just as frustrated. "She's sailing to Canada, too deaf for radio questioning and four days away from the nearest port."

Sherlock wouldn't be soothed, not even with a kiss.

"There'll be another murder if we can't crack this, John."

Think, Sherlock admonished himself. *You're meant to be bright.*

70. Conductor of Light

Sherlock withdrew from my touches, calling them unearned. Like somehow he was undeserving of my affection.

"Okay," I said, ignoring his mood, "Let's review it." I opened my sketch of Liam O'Rourke, redrawn from memory in greater detail. "The Professor's twin. How does Moriarty fit?"

"He's the architect," Sherlock said at once. "His expertise is in applied mathematics, with emphasis on game theory. I've suspected an organising force behind numerous unsolved high-value crimes over the last five years. Moriarty's our man."

"He's a genius, but O'Rourke's sly, and Moran's a thug. There's K-Jam. D'Angelo's murder…"

"O'Rourke's doing. Moran's auburn. The crime scene hairs were copper-red."

"So's Moriarty."

"Not his M.O. Moriarty lives discreetly well above his means. I suspect his inner circle of dubious post-graduate students do the grunt work."

"Dubious?"

"Two are scions of organised crime families. One was the late Melanie Porlock."

"Maybe that feeds into the bonds. He prints forgeries, sells them to these crimelords?"

Sherlock blinked; beamed. It made me feel like I'd been clever.

"Maybe you're not yourself luminous, John, but you're a conductor of light!"

"You may want to work on your compliments, love," I said wryly.

His surprise became contrition. "You reminded me. Game theory and auctions."

My heart sang when, before leaving, Sherlock kissed me devotedly, passionately, a promise of future delicious bawdiness.

71. Bidding War

Sherlock visited me with a theory and new, less brash, self-assurance. Watson wasn't mentioned, but evidence of fervent kissing confirmed his relationship's vitality.

We discussed Sherlock's theory. Intelligence anomalies from across Her Majesty's security services, previously thought inconsequential or erroneous, made new sense in light of Moriarty's game theory expertise.

Assiduous delving revealed his hidden wealth: London flat, country residence; numerous boats, including a luxury yacht, *Gemini*, recently launched.

Conclusion: Moriarty, having restricted supply, would offer what remained to buyers—from local crime organisations to more political groups. Counterfeit US bonds have value in both wealth creation and economic destabilisation.

My position in the British Government is unique. While my influence is not absolute, department heads take my counsel seriously. Representatives from the Metropolitan Police, MI5 and MI6 gathered as requested.

Professor Moriarty, on no-one's radar until then, had planned an All Pay Auction. Criminal parties would all pay, the winner selected by lottery. The deal would happen soon, at sea, if those curious anomalies fitted together as I believed.

Our operation was executed with commendable haste. *Gemini*, hosting the auction in the North Sea's international waters, was intercepted, attendees and evidence caught in the net.

But Moriarty wasn't there. O'Rourke was wounded in gunfire. He and Moran fled on a motorboat, but not before Moran killed MI6's valiant Agent Bradstreet.

72. Dual Nature

"They sent Bruiser Barron, John! Finally, this league of redheads is against the ropes."

We'd been ambushed at our door by a known thug-for-hire, but Sherlock was laughing with delight. Blood in his teeth, on his knuckles, his forehead.

I cleaned his split lip; checked that the fine bones of his hand weren't broken when he'd snatched Barron's weapon mid-attack. He'd jabbed Barron in the ribs with it before the bastard fled, then Sherlock dropped like a stone.

I examined the swelling on Sherlock's forehead; shone a penlight into his eyes.

"I'm fine," Sherlock said.

"I'll tell you if you're fine."

As I threw the bloodied gauze into the dish, my hand shook.

I've held men's ruptured flesh together with my own hands; sutured shrapnel wounds; treated the bloody stumps of bomb-severed limbs. My hands never shook before today.

"*In arduis fidelis*," Sherlock said softly. "You to a T."

Faithful in adversity. The RAMC motto.

I kissed his brow, calmer. "You're fine."

I know I'm a contradiction. A doctor who went to war. The veteran who convalesced by partnering with a detective. An ordinary man bored with the ordinariness of life.

And I swear, oath be damned, if Sherlock's wounds had been worse, I'd have pitched Barron into the street and made him fucking *eat* those nunchakus for *daring* such brutality.

73. Three Plans

Seb	Liam	James
How's the arm?		
	Hurts like fuck.	
		They'll pay.
Least I shot the prick who shot you.		
	Fuck this. I'm coming home.	
Keep your head down, Liam.		Not till I say so.
Hate to agree, but do as the Prof says.		
	Traitor.	
I'm a realist. I don't know how, but that prick Holmes has eyes everywhere. Stay put till we know you're clear.		
		I know how. He's recruited an army.
WTAF?	*What the fuck?*	
		An army of irregulars. Friends of that doctor of his. A network of veterans all over the city, including that pest you failed comprehensively to drown.

Fucking buggery shitballs. The little fuck.		
	You kiss our mam with that mouth?	
		So stay put until I know what eyes are on you. I want to be sure I can extract you unseen. Then you'll have to lie low. Poland. Or Norway.
Fucking Poland? Have you already got a plan?	*Fucking Norway? Have you got a plan, J?*	
		I have three. Testing them for weaknesses now.
Then *use* one of them!		
	Ease up Seb.	
You always take his side.		
	I don't.	
Just because you're bloody twins.		
	I don't always take his side.	
You do.		
		You do, Liam. But not because we're twins.

Why then?		
	Because, Seb, he is head of the League. He's the brains. We're the brawn.	

74. Unsung Hero

29 April

Don't think J realises everything he did.

Barron went for J first; blow to his diaphragm before striking my ribs. J went down (feared briefly J stabbed). Didn't quite dodge B's elbow (split my lip) but J thank god rose when the edge of B's nunchaku cut my brow. Sound of the sticks colliding must have sounded to J like my skull cracking.

The <u>sound</u> John made. Primal rage. Barron will have five perfect bruises where J death-gripped his left arm; I captured nunchaku in B's right hand, struck back. B tried to kick me. J kicked B's thigh & - only word for it is *roared* in B's ear. Blood-curdling. <u>Thrilling</u>.

Terrifying! B fled. I swear J'd have caught & thrashed him only vertigo brought me down. Head hit harder than I'd realised.

Slightest tremor in J's hand after. I've never known him afraid, till yesterday. For <u>me</u>.

Slept fitfully. J kept checking me for concussion. Pretended his own blackly bruised chest didn't hurt.

"Let me kiss it better anyway."

Managed the right tone. He relaxed, even laughed. Let me. (He tried not to wince. Wished I could truly make this better. But he sighed like it did.)

He reciprocated. So gentle on each bruise, beside each cut.

It…felt better.

How curious and wonderful to know I'm beloved.

75. Friesland

Egg sent word that a new Irregular, Cal Wiggins, spotted Moran slipping out of a Gravesend rifle club. Wiggins had stalked Moran to a flat-topped barge moored opposite Tilbury Fort.

"And away wi' Cluedo's wee fee," Egg added, "I'm havin' a grand time fer free."

Sherlock and John (bruised still) joined Wiggins at the jetty. The barge had winch housing at one end for its marine construction work, four shipping containers atop the wooden decking at the other.

"He ain't come back," reported Wiggins, "But I reckon he's hopped over to that little Dorset Catalina that's leaving."

"Lestrade's on the way. John."

John followed Sherlock. They boarded the barge unimpeded. The winch housing was empty, containers undisturbed. Sherlock's brow furrowed.

"He's lured us here."

"If I was Sebastian Moran, I wouldn't wait for us to hit a tripwire." John grabbed Sherlock's hand and ran; they jumped together into the murky river just as the deck began to heave and fill the air with shards of metal and wood.

"You lost him," Lestrade snapped as Wiggins helped them onto land, the *Friesland* a smoking wreck behind them.

"We found him," contradicted Sherlock.

Wiggins nodded. "He's on the *Judas Kiss*. It idled in remote detonation range and chugged off. The Irregulars are tracking it."

Sherlock grinned through his bruises, "The hook is baited."

76. Ex Family

"You have a client," Ellie Hudson reported as Sherlock and John returned from Tilbury. "Her kid's with her."

John climbed the stairs behind Sherlock, wishing all clients to hell. A hot shower, tea with rum. A quick check of any new bruises, a snuggle on the sofa before retiring to the bedroom for we-survived-an-exploding-barge celebratory orgasms. *That's* what they needed. Not clients.

John was entirely unprepared for the people waiting for them. His heart lurched.

The girl spoke first, tone surly-tremulous. "Remember me?"

"As if I could forget." John's warm smile was suffused with regret. "You look well."

The girl shrugged.

"I'm sorry I missed your birthday. I don't have your address. Happy thirteenth." John leaned in to hug the girl, maybe kiss her cheek. He halted at the girl's wounded look.

"Hi, John." The woman didn't rise; her hands remained folded in her lap.

"Mary," he replied stiffly

"Tea?" offered Sherlock, managing primness despite his bruising.

"Sorry Sherlock, I should've…um. This is Mary Morstan. My ex-wife. And m—her daughter. Alice."

"I've only just heard about Hugh," Mary said. "I'm so sorry."

"Well. It's hardly a surprise."

"No."

"How did you find me?"

"I bumped into Tom Stamford."

"Right."

Mary looked down to her lap. Alice assessed John and Sherlock moodily from under her fringe.

"Mary's getting remarried," Sherlock blurted.

77. Longing

Sherlock fled to the kitchen. He hadn't meant to unceremoniously declare his deduction, but after Tilbury, his mind raced as frantically as his heart.

John's *ex-wife*. John's *daughter*.

Why am I so discomposed? Their existence wasn't secret.

Mary Morstan had avoided the guest chairs to sit with her back to the window, face masked in shadow. Right hand over the left in her lap, concealing the ring on her finger. The shine of engagement diamond rather than wedding gold. Hidden. *Why?*

Sherlock noisily filled the kettle, fetched crockery, listened to them: John sincerely wishing her well; Mary describing her fiancé as a good man; a good father.

"Good," John said, like saying it hurt.

Alice, older than the likenesses John drew, had her mother's dark hair and blue eyes. Chin, ears, nose, willowy physique: not Mary's; nothing like John's.

John wasn't Alice's biological father.

Alice suddenly stood at his elbow. "You're John's boyfriend?"

"Yes," Sherlock confirmed evenly.

"You kiss 'n stuff?"

"Yes."

"So do Mum and Drew." Alice frowned. "Mr Stamford said John got shot and nearly died."

"Yes." *Do better.* "But he's fine now."

"Who bashed you?" Nodding at his forehead and lip.

"A thug. John intervened."

"Good." Alice sighed. "Drew's okay, but I still wish John was my real dad."

So does John, Sherlock realised. *Fatherhood isn't just biology.*

78. Do what you can with what you have

After Mary and Alice left, John downed a dram of whisky, then another.

At a loss for what to say, Sherlock stayed the third pour, his hand on John's.

John trailed his fingers over Sherlock's bruised knuckles.

"Close call today," said John.

"Yes."

"Will Moran bite?"

"He's getting desperate. He'll bite."

"Hmm." John moodily sipped his whisky.

"She's observant," Sherlock ventured. "Your Alice."

"She's not mine." Clipped.

"She loves you, though."

"I've no rights. I never formally adopted her." John's sorrow was palpable; Sherlock cursed himself for prying.

"I always had to be the good son, because Hugh was such a fuck-up," John continued. "Mary's parents were unforgivingly strict. We were both suffocating; I guess it made us natural allies. So we dated. Kissed. Said we were saving ourselves for marriage. When a church 'friend' got Mary pregnant; we got married and lived with my Dad while I studied. The day the midwife put Alice in my arms, that baby girl was mine."

John's eyes glittered with emotion. "Except she wasn't. Suddenly Alice wasn't my daughter any more, however many letters I wrote her. Now she's going to be someone else's."

Sherlock didn't know what to say, so he took John's hand. John immediately laced their fingers together.

"John…"

"Let's focus on what I *can* do. Let's get this arsehole bomber."

79. The Empty Houseboat

Seb's phone pinged. It'd just be bloody James again, all 'leave Holmes to me', 'I know best', blah blah blah.

Being a clever shite hadn't kept their make-a-fortune deal from going tits-up. Clever dickery had got Liam shot. Mam'd be fecking *furious*.

Seb meant to do for Holmes, then look after Liam. He'd pinched James' boat (*Judas Kiss? Christ* that boy had issues). Kept on the move. Done without sleep (or bathing). Plans A (Barron) and B (*Friesland*) had fizzled, but Seb had back-up plans.

This rendezvous in Elmley Nature Reserve was one.

Seb guided *Judas Kiss* to an aging landing, part-cluttered by a small, half-sunken houseboat. On the bank stood friend-of-a-dodgy-friend, Gordon 'Jeeves' Butler. Problem gambler, arse-kisser. Seb's for 10K. A *proper* Judas.

Seb, armed, stood on the bow.

"Got the cash?" Jeeves shouted.

Seb lobbed him a plump sports bag. "Half now; half after."

Jeeves peeked inside the bag. "Wait in the alley behind The Stormy Petrel tonight. I'll slip 'em both roofies. Easy-peasy."

Then he flung the cash-bag back to Seb, who automatically caught it, gun lowered.

That's when two armed men leapt onto the landing from the derelict houseboat. Their warning shots fixed Seb to the spot. Jeeves, the skeevy shite, grinned. Arse-kisser, yeah, but not Seb's.

It wasn't a surprise, but it was still a betrayal.

80. Reggie

Jeeves did well. We all know he's a bit shady, but K-Jam's his mate. Nobody messes with Jeeves' mates.

Sherlock remained troubled.

"Moriarty's the clever one, and he's vanished with O'Rourke."

"You'll work it out."

Sherlock gave me a curious sideways look. "And if I can't?"

"Then nobody can."

"You really think that, don't you? And you would…forgive me for failing."

"Nobody's perfect all the time." I couldn't help a smile. "You're close enough for me." I slid my arms around him; he wound himself around me too, pressed his crotch to my thigh, snugged between his legs.

We fell into bed, eager, delighted, everything heightened by a sudden new sense of freedom in Sherlock. He laughed, playfully nipped and sucked, blew raspberries on my bum.

Oh god, the gorgeous sounds he made, truly un-shy. I came so hard, so *loud*. He was devilishly smug.

Afterwards, cradled in my arms, Sherlock told me about Reggie Musgrave, who used him to solve a family mystery and never loved Sherlock at all. About the years of cocaine after, and abandoning it when it didn't help.

I laced my fingers through his. Kissed his face, fingers, shoulders. "I'm so glad you did." Kissed his hair; breathed him in.

Distraught, after the fact, that I could have lost him.

A thought not to be borne.

81. Curiouser and Curiouser

Alice sits sullen-stubborn at the table where Ms Hudson put her, when John's boyfriend, Sherlock, enters.

He pretends he's not surprised.

"I myself like a cup of tea after a long journey," he says, putting on the kettle.

John arrives with the mail. He's *proper* shocked.

"Alice came all alone from Exmouth by train," announces Sherlock.

"It wasn't *hard*," Alice scoffs.

"Does Mary know you're here?" John asks.

Alice scowls.

"I'll call," says Sherlock and leaves.

"What's wrong?" John does his Doctor Voice.

"Nothing." She means to be angry but all her unhappiness tumbles out. "I don't *know* anyone. And Drew's got *so many rules*. He doesn't like kids. And school's *stupid*, and you went away and you stayed away and you nearly died and *I miss you*."

She's crying as John holds her hands and kisses her forehead.

"I miss you too."

"No you don't. You didn't want a stupid kid either."

She's satisfied and horrified by his distress.

"Alice. No. You're my Wondergirl. Leaving you was my only regret, but I'm not…The law says I'm not your dad."

She's sobbing now.

John presses her folded hands to his chest. Over his heart. "But in here, I am. Always, Alice. Always. Hush."

Then she's sheltered in her father's arms, tearful but safe.

For now.

Her Mum's going to go ballistic.

82. Tea Party

Alice is waaaay too old for tea parties, but they've made such a *production* out of it. Fine china, milky tea, honeyed crumpets, cucumber sandwiches, and devilled eggs, her favourite.

Okay, so it's kinda fun.

"Anything you *do* like about Exmouth?" John asks.

"Guitar lessons," announces Sherlock. He waggles his own fingers, displaying violin calluses; turns her hands to reveal similar marks. "New since last visit. You practise daily."

"I thought you were magic. That's just a trick," she teases.

"My method never amazes once it's explained." His expression is tragic!

"I still think you're amazing." John quick-kisses Sherlock's lips.

"Gross!" Alice protests, but honestly, they're adorkable.

Sherlock looks at John like he's made of stars. (Drew looks at Mum like that. Maybe he's not all bad.)

The doorbell rings. One minute later: "*Alice Grace Morstan! What were you thinking?*"

Alice guiltily endures the angry-relieved lecture. Mum really was scared.

Sherlock solemnly shakes Alice's hand; gives her his business card. "In case mysteries need solving. Even though it's only a trick."

"It's a *brilliant* trick."

He sunshine-smiles.

John hugs Alice goodbye super-hard. Holds Sherlock's hand super-tight after.

Driving home, Mum says: "I was wrong to let us lose touch. John misses you too. He'd like you to visit. Be good and I'll consider it."

Alice promises, already planning the half-term break.

83. Sly Getaway

At 11pm, light flashed three times in his window. Liam O'Rourke, wounded arm bandaged, left his hideaway: clean-shaven, hair dyed brown, wrapped in a coat, hunched to conceal his height, walking differently.

This wasn't Liam's first sly getaway.

He rejected two cabs; entered the third. "Trafalgar Square."

At the square, he crossed to the Uber waiting on the other side.

"About bloody time," he said, getting in. "Thought I'd die there of old age."

"Hmm," said the driver, muffled in scarf and hat as he pulled into traffic.

"And now I have to go to fecking *Switzerland*."

"Hmm."

"I hate Switzerland."

The car swung off the road into a smaller street.

"I hate Trafalgar Square too. That Fourth Plinth's fecking rubbish again."

"I liked the Blue Cock," said the driver, stopping in a tiny mews.

Alarmed, Liam lunged awkwardly for the door, but a police detective barred the way. Liam resisted, but, injured, was easily subdued.

"How?" he demanded, confused and enraged.

"The delivery of first aid supplies for treating gunshots," said another man, arriving from nowhere, "from a pharmacist with several observant veterans as clients."

"Your fucking spies," Liam cursed.

"Arranging lookouts, three cabs and an Uber was easy." The Uber driver kissed that newcomer's cheek.

Liam recognised them and cursed: the damned Earl's Court tube artist and violin busker.

84. Graveside

I visited Hugh's grave with scotch in one hand, flowers in the other.

I hadn't even begun to organise a headstone for him. Months yet to decide on that.

I put the flowers beside the grass marker. Sat. Opened the scotch.

"Cheers, Hugh, you bastard."

I poured a measure into the earth, took a swig.

"I'm sorry," I said.

I downed another dram. Poured Hugh's next measure into the dirt.

"Mary's happier without either of us. Probably just as well I caught you kissing. I think I'd have forgiven you sooner, if that mess hadn't cost me Alice."

A drink for me. A drink for Hugh.

"You were right to call me coward about staying in the closet. Getting shot helps you understand your priorities. Maybe if you'd survived this overdose, you'd have done better. I wish I could've saved you. I'm so sorry I stopped trying."

Swallow. Pour.

"I miss how we used to be when we were young. Before Mum died. "

Swallow. Pour.

"I'm in love, Hugh. Madly. If there's an afterlife, and you don't hate me, help me to not screw this up too."

I patted the grass growing over him. "Goodbye, big brother. I wish we'd done better."

Then, because it couldn't hurt him any more, or me, I left him the rest of the bottle.

85. Declaration of War

Professor James Moriarty's fury at his brothers' capture was an ice storm: arctic and seething.

Moriarty was always a cipher to those around him. And why not? Abandoned as a baby, his mother's name placed only on Liam's papers, he lost name and family, both. Once fostered, James O'Rourke vanished.

The Moriartys were more intent on moulding him than knowing him. Their parental cuddles and kisses were wielded as rewards, withheld as punishment. With them, the first of many layers was laid over his true self. Bricked behind a wall of being no-one and having nothing but his mind.

He'd bent cold thought to finding his real family. He rediscovered Liam and half-brother Sebastian the Thug. Liam loved Seb, though, so James tolerated him.

Now his brothers were arrested; their budding consulting criminal empire was collapsing. All his plans and schemes only ruins and dust.

Moriarty wrote to Sherlock Holmes. Good, old-fashioned pen on paper; from the soon-to-be-abandoned university address.

Stand down, Holmes. You're an entertaining opponent but I'm no longer amused. Free my brothers or I'll end you.

Foolishly incriminating, but James had multiple plans. Incarceration was none of them.

Holmes' succinct postcard reply: *Many have said so, yet here I am. Bring it.*

James Moriarty, incognito, collected this insult from his pigeonhole, evaded the watching police—and swore bloodshed.

86. Down the Rabbit Hole

Mary called in the early afternoon, irritated. "Alice's taken off again."

"She's not here," I said. "Has there been a fight?"

"No more than usual," Mary sighed, exasperated.

"She's looking forward to visiting us. I don't think she'd jeopardise that."

"Where else would she go?"

My heart lurched. "How long's she been gone?"

"I found out she's not at school."

Sherlock emerged from the bathroom, wrapped in a towel. I was too distracted to appreciate him. (Damp Sherlock usually earns at least a kiss.) "John?"

"Alice skipped school today. Mary…"

"She'd be here by now if she was coming," Sherlock said sharply. He snatched his phone up from the table and began texting, finding clothes. "Ask Mary if anything odd occurred this week."

I asked.

"No! John, what's wrong?"

Sherlock anticipated the question.

"Moriarty swore payback. Alice's probably playing truant, but let's be certain. I've hired a car. Four hours to Exmouth. Tell Mary to advise the police. Ms Hudson will call if Alice surfaces here." He'd finished throwing on clothes. "Come on."

Mary was inclined to panic as I explained.

"She'll be fine," I asserted, stemming my own horror. *My little girl!* "She's probably with a friend."

We made it to Exmouth in three hours.

Alice wasn't with any friend. And she hadn't been seen since missing the school bus.

87. The Needle

I mustn't fail.

On reaching Exmouth, Sherlock bee-lined for Birchwood Road, where Alice was last seen walking towards Exmouth Community College. A 25-minute walk.

John won't forgive me. I won't forgive myself.

Would that distracted goodbye kiss as he left be their last, if he failed?

Sherlock's first useful witness said, "I saw her walking. Should've caught the bus." (Idiot)

He texted John: *Seen on Withycombe Village Rd.*

John was tracing Alice's probable path from the College end. The police thought they were overreacting. (Idiots.)

Do better.

A blind woman sat in her little garden, enjoying the evening air.

"I heard a man offer someone a lift," she said. "A girl told him to fuck off. I heard a loud thump, then maybe a splash. He drove off, fast."

Moments later, Sherlock examined the nearby road crossing Withycombe Brook, a narrow gush of water corralled behind houses.

Alice's phone glistened in the shallow water. He scrambled down.

Failure ends on the point of a needle.

Smeared algae. Blood on the culvert. She'd tried to climb out. Couldn't.

"*Alice!*"

He ran, following the trail of her attempts.

Saw Alice, legs submerged. He *ran.*

"J-J-John?"

"He's coming," Sherlock promised.

He texted John; called 999. He gently removed Alice from the water; kept her warm.

Sherlock was appalled, enraged. Oddly reassured. Moriarty had *blundered*.

88. Through the Looking Glass

Alice shivers, but John's boyfriend's wrapped his coat around her. He's holding her; her head on his chest. She feels safe. (He even smells a bit like John. Is that John's shirt?)

"*Alice?!*" Alice and Sherlock both tilt their heads to watch John splashing up the culvert. An ambulance wails nearby. John still gets here first.

"Her ankle's broken," Sherlock explains, "Her head's bruised. Pulse fine, bleeding's stopped."

Doctor John examines her. "Possible concussion." He kisses her hair. "I've got you, baby girl."

The ambulance arrives, and Mum, who gets in with her. John's not allowed. (He's not officially her dad.)

Alice is mildly concussed and it's even more boring than it looks on crime shows. Her ankle's in plaster.

It's funny what bothers you when you're hurt. Since she fell in the brook, she's been preoccupied with what Tom told her. So when John visits, Alice asks what she shouldn't.

"Does it hurt? Where you got shot?"

(When she was little, John would ask, "Where does it hurt, Wondergirl?" and he'd make it better.)

She thinks he won't answer (he hates upsetting her). "Not any more," he says. "I'm good now."

Alice squeezes his hand. Whispers. "Good. Me too."

She's sleepy. As she dozes, John draws a mouse on her cast, then holds her hand and sings songs by Beyoncé.

89. Waiting Game

"Moriarty made a mistake."

"You bet he fucking did. I'll kill him."

Sherlock didn't try to placate me. "It won't be necessary, but if I'm wrong, I'll be your alibi."

I stared.

"He overstepped his capacity," Sherlock said now that I'd stopped pacing. "He's an exemplary planner, a genius in the field of game theory, but he overreached himself. He's become irrational. He could have simply shot her from the car—"

I flinched.

"—if all he wanted was revenge. Ah. Sorry John. But it's true. Instead, he made sure Alice could identify him. It's a message: he wants his brothers, and will hurt us through family if he doesn't get them."

His theory was logical but unhelpful. My hands shook with wanting to beat that fucker bloody for hurting my little girl.

"If he dares—"

"Alice is safe," Sherlock insisted. "Apart from the police presence, the failed counterfeit bonds auction has brought international players on board. MI5 agents are protecting Alice at the hospital. With the CIA, they're staking out the university, Moriarty's boats, his flat and country house, and all departure points."

"He'll be in hiding."

"He'll come out. Game theory is not hostage negotiation."

Sherlock said it like a promise, sealed it with a kiss on my trembling fist.

"Mycroft and I have set the bait."

90. And the Damage Done

Sherlock's planned end to the Musgrave Ritual became a catastrophe when John returned early, and saw its instruments laid out on the table. Syringe. Fresh needle. The last dose of cocaine.

"What the fuck?"

Had John been horrified, hurt, Sherlock might have explained. But John was enraged. He thought he knew what this was.

It's not that. Why can't you see that's not what this is?

"Answer me, Sherlock."

Sherlock's panic became anger at being so judged. John was supposed to *know* him.

Furious, Sherlock withdrew into scornful emotional distance, always his defence in the years before John, against people like Reggie; how he'd kept Mycroft away from his shame.

"My mind's like a racing engine. Without occupation it tears itself to pieces."

"You're shooting up because you're *bored*? Bullshit. Don't tell me the brightest mind I know can't invent ways to stave off boredom. Hugh was an inventive liar too."

"Spare me the sanctimony."

But at Hugh's name, the despair had risen up behind John's fury.

Oh god. Hugh.

Sherlock wanted to recall his cold words; to apologise, explain, be forgiven with a kiss.

But John had stormed out, choking on horror, slamming the door shut behind him.

Leaving Sherlock speechless, the shock of it a gravity well, swallowing sound. Devouring hope.

He stood frozen: heart desolated; of ideas, barren.

91. Desertion

The silence in Baker Street pressed on Sherlock's ears. It had the mass and bulk of *permanence*.

He'd learned a lot about John in their time together, after all.

Was that time at an end now? Precedent suggested yes. John had fled his closeted sexuality into a doomed marriage. He'd fled a ruined marriage into the army. He'd walked away from an irredeemable brother into isolation. He'd been ejected from a destroyed career to fall into Sherlock's orbit at Baker Street.

Discovering Sherlock with a needle and a seven percent solution had sent John running again.

John was not coming back.

Except that he did; not five minutes after storming out.

John flung the door open and stood on the threshold; wet eyes red-rimmed; breathing laboured and swift like a panicking bird.

Sherlock stood exactly where he had since John had left; immobilised by the logical conclusion of John's leaving.

"I'm sorry," said John. His voice was as ragged as his appearance. He was defeated and determined and struck down by grief. "I shouldn't have walked out just now. I'm not doing that again."

"You're not leaving?" The kiss of hope stirred Sherlock's mind to life again.

"No. I'm done running, Sherlock. We're going to sort this out. I love you and I'm staying right here with you. Where I belong."

92. A New Conclusion

Sherlock didn't remember folding, but he was hands-and-knees on the floor, hyperventilating.

"Don't cry." But John was crying too, falling to his knees, wrapping his arms around Sherlock.

"I'm staying right here," John promised, kissing his hair. "Whatever it takes, Sherlock. I'll help if I can. I'll stay with you even if I can't. Even if you tell me to go. We'll work through this. I won't lose you to this poison."

Sherlock drew a steadying breath. "Wrong deduction."

John bristled in his confusion. Sherlock hastened to clarify.

"I haven't used in years. Five years 70 days, to be exact."

"Thank Christ." Relief.

"You're right. I'm not bored." Sherlock mustered his courage. "I've been reliably informed that barring my deductive skills, I'm...tedious. Of neither use nor ornament." A pained smile. "Cocaine became my solution to discovering I'm inherently dull."

"You? That's bullshit."

"Finally, I began to question Reggie's conclusion. Between cases I used to contemplate the matter, fearing he was right. Reminding myself he shouldn't matter. I realised recently he doesn't. I planned to destroy those things today."

"Good."

"You don't need me to solve crimes to maintain your interest, do you?" Less a statement; more a plea.

John, solemn, cupped Sherlock's face in his strong hands.

"You're the best and wisest man I know," John said, "And Reggie's a bell-end."

93. Declaration of Love

I saw the needle and had to leave, suffocating in grief.

But leaving made it worse.

I'll stand by him then, and suffocate, I decided. *I'll stay till the bitterest of ends if there's any chance I'll save him.*

Only I was wrong again. Thank god. *Thank fucking god.* Terrible timing, to find him with that paraphernalia on the day he'd decided to destroy it.

Sherlock finally told me the whole of how Musgrave had used him; how cruelly that bastard treated him when Sherlock didn't find gold.

Sherlock smashed the syringe with a hammer. He emptied the cocaine into the sink, washed it away with boiling water. We took the needle to Tom Stamford at St Bart's for disposal. Bless him for questioning nothing.

"I lost myself for a while," Sherlock said later, in Postman's Park. "Buried the pain in cocaine. Decided it made me interesting. But I'd only made Reggie right."

I kissed his fingers, held his wrist to my cheek to feel his blessed pulse.

I *detest* Reginald Musgrave.

I cried. I thought I'd lost Sherlock, like I've lost everybody else.

"I'm sorry," he said.

I studied the plaques to dead and unsung heroes.

"I love you," I said.

Sherlock, damp cheek pressed to mine, whispered against my ear: "I love you too. Heart, mind, body and breath."

94. Lure

James Moriarty had never been so angry in his life. And he'd spent most of his life incensed.

Give my brothers back to me.

Fuck the job, the boats, the flat. Fuck the money. He could make money; buy better things. Once that interfering arsehole Sherlock Holmes was dead.

First he needed Liam back, and that idiot Seb. Surprising to find it wasn't only Liam who loved the grubby reprobate. Moriarty would kiss both the halfwit's sallow cheeks, the minute he freed his brothers.

I'll take *my brothers back. Or send everyone to hell.*

James now applied the rat cunning he'd observed in Seb with more considered calculation.

He knew Holmes' weaknesses.

The doctor; anyone to do with him. (Step one: misdirection.)

Moriarty allowed one of Holmes' Irregulars to spot him skulking around the Heath in his van. (Step two: foster underestimation.)

Holmes' brother Mycroft, almost a recluse, only moved to and from his flat in Pall Mall to his office in Whitehall. A short but vulnerable walk. (Step Three: the unexpected.)

It'd been easy to drive at the girl; make her jump off a bridge.

Turned out easy, too, to wrest a fat bureaucrat into the van and use the fatty's phone to send a message.

I've got your brother.

You've got two of mine.

Let's swap. 6am.

Thames Barrier.

95. The Odyssey

I'd hoped to make it difficult for Professor Moriarty to manhandle me. A man of my bulk refusing to move requires some handling, especially with only cloud-scudded moonlight for illumination.

The pistol he produced was even more quelling than expected when accompanied by, "No reason for him to get you back unharmed, you know."

Moriarty banked on our obligation to be civil, and not commit eye-for-an-eye retribution.

Perforce, I must obey him. I climbed gracelessly into his stolen yellow motorboat, wrists tied behind me. He steadied me as I swayed. Injured I may be of value, of none if drowned.

I dreaded disembarkation, but he weighed anchor by span G of the Thames Barrier, presently devoid of river traffic. The Plough in Ursa Major and the Pole Star indicated it was 5am.

"Any last words for your wretched brother?"

Unnecessarily ominous, or simply bombast. I remained silent, only part-feigning fear. I appreciate stars from my attic telescope; I deplored being so exposed beneath them.

In the darkness, bobbing on the tide, I recited Homer in Greek, a distraction from seasickness, and trusted in my brother.

Sunrise kissed the tailfins of London City's incoming planes; washed the Thames silver-orange as another motorboat approached. Sherlock (virtually alone, as instructed) stood amidships. Watson directed the rudder.

The redheaded murderers sat smugly in the bow.

96. The Fall

16 May

- *Flowers (John) (Inadequate thanks)*
- *Flowers (Mycroft)*

What idiot on the Barrier gave away MI5's position? Reflection off a lens? A scuffling foot?

When M realised the trap, he pushed Myc (anxious, seasick, bound) overboard. (<u>Not</u> in the plan! We knew M's attack on Alice a diversion; knew he'd target Mycroft—but *drown* him?)

M shot at me.

Slow to move (shock!), John tackled me. Bullet practically parted my hair!

J didn't wait. Dived in. M *shot* at him. <u>*Arse*</u>.

I pulled Moran & O'Rourke (roped together) to deck, grabbed motor, drove straight at M. Collided. M shot the motor; <u>boarded</u> us, still shooting.

O'Rourke yelled to stop; M wouldn't. O'Rourke shouldered into him; both went overboard. I held Moran (still attached) & tried to drag O'Rourke back. M's grip too tight. He finally sank, but O'Rourke beyond saving.

Met/MI5 finally acted; hauled John & Mycroft out of Thames. Confused idea J kissing him, till Mycroft coughed up half the river.

My poor, beloved brother isn't made for fieldwork.

Moran howled for his brothers. Mine survived, thanks to John.

M's machinations led only to the permanence of the final problem: *is there an afterlife?*

I doubt it. The better resolution—survivor of my ritual—*do better*. In myriad ways, but Mycroft & John are inspirations always to be my best.

97. Where the Heart Is

Two dead. I couldn't help thinking of them as The Enemy. Not good for someone who's a civilian doctor now, but better them than Sherlock or his brother.

I accompanied Mycroft in the ambulance. Poor man clung to my hand, demanding reassurance that Sherlock was unharmed. I could promise him that. The cheeky bugger had blown a kiss up to me on the barrier gate. All bravado, ghost pale.

Eventually Sherlock joined us at the hospital, pretending unsuccessfully not to fret.

Lungfuls of Thames water is never good for a man, but Mycroft's doctors declared him relatively unscathed. Sherlock visited him briefly but only calmed a little.

Sherlock must have been as strung out as I was. That bastard Moriarty nearly shot him, for fuck's sake. At home, he stripped me, not in passion but anxiety, searching for fresh injuries. Finding none, frantic kisses followed.

We held tight, brought frantic down to luxuriously slow.

"You reek of the Thames," Sherlock said, half laughing, half not.

"You really have to work on those compliments, love."

We laughed then. Undressed. In the shower, we washed each other's hair, skin. Hands all over each other, then between. Breathing hard, crying out, then sighing soft. Alive. *Together.*

Later in bed, he laughed at my fond foolishness as I drew hearts over his chest in biro.

98. Sigerson

Meet me at the Langham.
I'm under the name of Sigerson.
John was texting as he moved: "On my way!"
The hotel lift took John to the third floor. He stepped into dove grey and cream furnishings. A subtle carpet led to an understated door.

'Sigerson' reclined on the sumptuous bed in white shirt and dark trousers, hands folded behind his head. Barefoot, he wriggled his toes, grinned impishly. His knees fell open, the better to present evidence of his arousal.

John's gaze dragged slow from the soles of Sherlock's feet, up long legs, splayed knees, to burgeoning erection. Up waist and chest to dark nipples, pebbled, visible through fine cotton. His gaze lingered on throat, lips, eyes.

"Sigerson?"

"An explorer."

"I see."

"In the mood to be explored."

John's knowing grin was sultry; hungry. "Might take a while. To explore. Thoroughly."

"We have all night, courtesy of a grateful Scandinavian monarch."

"You could advertise 'by appointment'." John was removing shoes, jacket.

"If it wasn't a secret."

"Mmm." John knelt at the end of the bed; caressed Sherlock's feet; lifted each arch to kiss in turn. He crawled along Sherlock's body, untucking the shirt with his teeth. He tongued nipples, sucked that throat. Kissed Sherlock's panting mouth.

A fortnight beyond Moriarty; a year beyond individual despair, they re-consummated their new beginning.

99. Storybook Ending

Alice Morstan	John Watson
OMG!! YOU MADE A BOOK FOR ME!!!!	
	Only one of its kind :D
I can't believe you wrote all of this!!	
	Well thanks. :/
:-p	
	I told you stories when you were little.
But you never *wrote* them. And these ones are true!	
	Mostly. Sherlock says I've embellished some too much.
:-p to Sherlock. I ♥ the clockwork bee one! Your pictures are beee-yooooo-tiful!! Mum reckons it'd be a bestseller.	
	Sherlock likes the art best. ☺
The hands you drew on the cover are his, right? And the eyes?	
	Spot on! Did you see yourself?
The little mouse with the sword!	
	That's you. My brave girl.
I wasn't *that* brave.	
	*You're *very* brave. I'm proud of you.*
Mum says I can still come visit you for break.	

I'd rather have adventures.

Maybe more like clockwork bee & fishtank adventures though. Run-over-by-cars adventures suck.

I know. But can we have a *little* adventure? PLEEEEEEEEEAAAAAAAA AAAAAAAAAASE!!!!

They go next week! PLEEEEEEEEEAAAAAAAA AAAAAAAAAASE!!!!

You're the best! :-* :-* :-*

You're funny! And thanks again for my gorgeous book!

I've promised her you'll be safe.

Really?

Sherlock's brother agrees with you. But you're both okay now. You know you're safe here, right?

Maybe a little one. If you're off the crutches.

If something comes up, and your mum agrees, and Sherlock.

You're better!

100. Art in the Blood

"Mycroft sent apologies, and flowers."

"That's good of him. Oh god, I'm nervous."

"Don't be."

"You think the book's rubbish."

"I never said that. I said you've made exercises in logic into swashbuckling romances appreciated best by readers of *The Guardian*."

"Well, sorry."

"Oh, John. No. My art's in deduction. Yours is in this splendid book. You're a romantic—"

"Says the man who made me breakfast in bed today, presented with a rose."

"Everyone loves your writing John, and your art. You'll be a huge success. Come here."

…

"Still think I'm the romantic one?"

"Do you want to talk or kiss?"

"Kiss."

…

"Oi, you pair! Still so handsy after a year!"

"K-Jam! Blue!"

"The other Irregulars are coming. Hey, Cluedo."

"Blue."

"Look at you two hooligans."

"DI Lestrade! Thanks for coming."

"Wouldn't miss your book launch, John! Especially since I'm in it."

"Jooooooooooooooooohn!"

"Oof! Easy, Alice!"

"You dedicated it to me!"

"Of course. The original's yours. Hi, Mary."

"Congratulations John."

"Ah, Ms Hudson…"

"You've met Marie?"

"My Ellie's chuffed to be in your book, Doc. She'll be the most famous non-speaking role in fiction, ever."

"Ah…"

"Speech time!"

"Thanks Blue. Ah, *fuck*."

"John. Breathe. Hold my hand."

"…I love you, Sherlock."

"I love you, too. Now, remember—"

"Use my notes."

"Yes. And that you're a talented badass."

About the artist and acknowledgements:
Caroline Jennings

Caroline Jennings has been drawing ever since her dad first showed her what a pencil was. Since then, she has worked in a variety of mediums but always comes back to her box of knackered old pencils and the pile of sketchbooks that she never seems to be able to fill. She hasn't won any awards for art since school and although it's just a hobby, she has illustrated several books and would be more than happy to do that for a living. Never before has she been asked to draw a clockwork bee.

Thank you to Narrelle for asking me to join this project in the first place. It was very liberating to draw as someone else for a little while and I have learned so much from that freedom, not least that drawing hands is still really, really hard. Narrelle has done an amazing job on these stories; each one is a lovingly crafted little jewel.

I'd also like to thank Atlin Merrick because she is a true force of nature and the single most encouraging human being I know. I've been very lucky to have her to kick me up the bum.

And of course, all the love to my family and to the core of my entire world, my husband Loren, and Callum, my beautiful little boy.

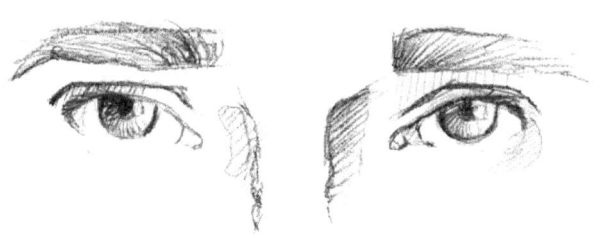

Acknowledgements:
Narrelle M Harris

My first thanks go to the clever writer(s) who first proposed the notion of the 221b ficlet, whoever they were. After writing 100 221bs within a story arc and within deadline, I don't know rightly whether to thank or curse them, but I wrote a book, so thanking is probably more appropriate.

Thanks go of course to Arthur Conan Doyle for creating these men and so many wonderful concepts that have endured for 130 years. He found his own creation problematic, had fewer than no damns to give about continuity, and famously told actor William Gillette, "You may marry him, murder him, or do anything you like to him." Writers have taken those words and run with them, to the joy of many.

My love and gratitude also go to Caroline Jennings, whose work I long admired. I was delighted that Caroline agreed to produce John's sketches to illustrate these stories! Aren't they wonderful?!

Thank you Atlin Merrick for thinking this was a good idea and for endless encouragement.

Thank you to my husband Tim Richards, my stalwart companion. I'd say the Watson to my Holmes except that I'm pretty sure he's the Holmes and I'm Watson.

So many effusive thanks go to Dimi, Janet and Wendy, for more reasons than I can count. With these friends, I am truly blessed.

About the author:
Narrelle M Harris

Narrelle M Harris writes crime, horror, fantasy, romance and erotica. Her 30+ novels and short stories have been published in Australia, US and UK. See narrellemharris.com for details.

Her award nominations include *Fly By Night* (Ned Kelly Award), *Witch Honour* and *Witch Faith* (both short-listed for the George Turner Prize), and *Walking Shadows* (Chronos Awards; Davitt Awards).

In 2017, her ghost/crime story *Jane* won the Athenaeum Library's Body in the Library prize at the Scarlet Stiletto Awards.

Narrelle's romances (het and queer) often combine romance with adventure/crime and have been published by Clan Destine Press, Manifold Press, Escape Publishing and Improbable Press. *The Adventure of the Colonial Boy* is a Holmes/Watson crime/romance set in 1893 Australia.

Narrelle also writes the traditional Holmes-and-Watson friendship, with adventures published in MX Publishing's *MX Book of New Sherlock Holmes Stories Volumes 5* and *6*, *Sherlock Holmes: The Australian Casebook*, and *Baker Street Irregulars: The Game is Afoot*.

Narrelle's queer paranormal thriller-romance, *Ravenfall*, was released in 2017 by Clan Destine Press.

Of her wide variety of genres, Narrelle says that her themes remain consistent.

"Whether you're reading a vampire adventure in modern Melbourne, a Holmesian mystery in London or a racy lesbian romance in the Middle East, you'll find themes of redemption and connection; you'll find humour and heart.

"And naturally, in my erotic romances, bottoms."

Also from Narrelle M Harris

1893. Dr Watson, still in mourning for the death of his great friend Sherlock Holmes, is now triply bereaved, with his wife Mary's death in childbirth. Then a telegram from Melbourne, Australia intrudes into his grief. "Come at once if convenient." Both suspicious and desperate to believe that Holmes may not, after all, be dead, Watson goes as immediately as the sea voyage will allow. Soon Holmes and Watson are together again, on an adventure through Bohemian Melbourne and rural Victoria, following a series of murders linked by a repulsive red leech and one of Moriarty's lieutenants. But things are not as they were. Too many words lie unsaid between the Great Detective and his biographer. Too much that they feel is a secret. Solve the crime, forgive a friend, rediscover trust and admit to love. Surely that is not beyond that legendary duo, Sherlock Holmes and Dr John Watson? Improbable Press books add romance to the adventure, set in a world where Sherlock Holmes and John Watson's relationship steps beyond friendship.

Some things belong together, the one with the other, natural pairs. Sherlock Holmes and John Watson. Holmes and Watson. Sherlock and John. Whether it's in an empty house during the Blitz, a West London strip club in the 70s, or deep in the heart of a Hong Kong computer lab, the meeting of these two legendary men is inevitable. Spanning one hundred and twenty-eight years, here are the stories of that destiny. Of how a detective meets a doctor, of how they change each other in heart and mind. Of how they fall in love.

Also from Improbable Press

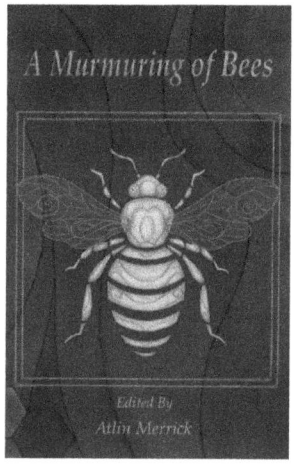

Think of Sherlock Holmes and you think of mysteries, John Watson...and bees. While Arthur Conan Doyle sent the great detective to tend hives in retirement, here bees are front and centre in stories of love and romance, war and hope, of honey on the tongue and a sting in the tail. In tales of rare nectars, secret diaries, and the private language of lovers, bees may be the buzzing heart of the story...or as ephemeral as a murmur. What you'll find in every tale are John Watson and Sherlock Holmes helping one another, wanting one another, loving one another. To encourage a world where such love is seen for the precious thing it is, profits from "A Murmuring of Bees" will be donated to the It Gets Better Project.

Lightning Source UK Ltd.
Milton Keynes UK
UKHW02f0532190618
324457UK00010B/410/P